The Right Brother

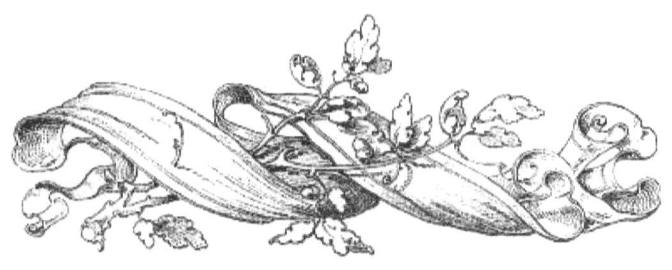

Tammy Mannersly

The Right Brother
Copyright © 2017 Tammy Mannersly

ISBN: (ebook) 978-1-945910-27-2
(print) 978-1-958136-47-8

Inkspell Publishing
207 Moonglow Circle #101
Murrells Inlet, SC 29576

Edited By Rie Langdon
Cover art By Najla Qamber

DEDICATION

To Rita, Ian and Leo.
Thank you for always encouraging me
to achieve my dreams.

TAMMY MANNERSLY

CHAPTER ONE

Davenport Residence. Five o'clock. The night of Christmas Eve.

"It's lovely to see you, Mr. Davenport," the elderly housekeeper chortled. "Your brother is in the study."

"Thanks, Margaret." Blake stepped over the threshold and into David's brightly lit, luxurious, beach-chic mansion. A white and gold marble staircase climbed to the second story before him, while the great lounge beyond the entry looked inviting in its hues of navy, onyx and pearl. Though he'd tried to sound sincere, he was not thrilled to be seeing his older brother so soon after their row. David thought he could buy everything, but a good woman's heart was never for sale.

Margaret closed the door behind Blake and ushered him through. "Merry Christmas," she reminded him as he left her for the pristine white walls and glorious, framed seascapes of the hall.

He nodded in appreciation, but still couldn't bring himself to smile. Blake hoped Gwen could see through his brother's chicanery. Christmas was a time for family, not for another one of his brother's schemes.

***

Gwen's nerves had her frozen at the lavish front door. Even at five-ten, the eight-foot-tall, dark oak double doors seemed to loom over her. Her stomach flip-flopped anxiously. She was about to spend Christmas week until New Year's with the family of one of her students. She had never done anything like it before, but David had been so charming. It had only been last week that David Davenport, multi-media mogul and single father of six-year-old Emily, had propositioned her with an offer she felt she couldn't refuse. Never in her life had she felt so special, as to have been singled out and chosen by a man as handsome and successful as David. With her friends and remaining family still back in Perth, she would've been alone again this Christmas, as she had the past two years, had it not been for the last-minute invite.

She smoothed the soft fabric of her short, paisley dress nervously. Her palms were already moist and her face flushed. It was a warm evening and she was still getting used to the heavy humidity of Queensland summers. Or that's what she was telling herself, anyway. The mere thought that she might be intimidated by the grandeur of the people and events that awaited her seemed to make matters worse. She knew she would stand out in David's world.

The Davenports' incredible canal-side mansion was in the glitzy heart of Noosa Heads, just west of Gwen's lonely studio apartment at Sunshine Beach. She had tried to quell her restless nerves on the drive over, but still found herself a slave to them. Her last relationship had put the fear of heartbreak into her and she had hidden her feelings away ever since. *But it's time now*, she vowed, as her slender finger poised over the doorbell. She had finally healed and felt as though she was ready to give love another chance. Though her short time with David had yet to ignite any feelings of desire within her, she owed it to herself, and to him, to give it a shot. David had been named one of Queensland's most eligible bachelors three years running before he married and now he shared that title with his brother. If she couldn't give someone as worthy as him the time of day, then maybe she really was better off alone. Shaking her head, she dismissed the thought away. She was ready. Her finger pressed against the doorbell. The delicate chiming of bells followed until Gwen began to question herself once more.

"Maybe this is a bad idea," she muttered. With fear getting the better of her, she turned on her heel and took a step toward the front path. At that moment, the Davenports' door opened.

"Yes, can I help you?" The kind tone of the housekeeper had Gwen turning around sheepishly.

"Yes. Sorry. My name is Gwen Deveraux. Mr. Davenport should be expecting me."

"Of course, dear. Please come in."

Gwen forced herself to take the leap and step inside. As she did so, a casually dressed man appeared from the hallway. Even with his stern expression, she recognized him from numerous magazine spreads she'd read. It was Blake, David's younger brother. She'd assumed his busy work schedule as one of Australia's most illustrious landscape photographers would have kept him away over the holiday period. She swallowed as her eyes drank in the sight of him. The images in the media didn't do him justice. His handsomeness was awe-inducing and his perfect appearance belonged in front of the camera, rather than behind it. As he strode toward her, all brooding eyes, dark hair, and taut muscle, her heart quickened its rhythm.

"We need to talk," he told her.

The smooth, deep octaves of his voice gave her goose bumps.

"We do?" Her voice escaped meekly in surprise as she mentally questioned his words.

***

Although Blake was riled after another curt disagreement with his brother, he found himself stunned by the beauty of David's newest interest. Over the past fortnight, he'd heard enough stories of Gwen to know that she was twenty-eight, Emily's primary school teacher and a loyal, kind-hearted innocent at risk of his brother's dishonest advances. Obviously, from what he saw in front of him, what he hadn't realized was just how captivating the tall, auburn-haired, green-eyed beauty was actually going to be. Her svelte body had tempting curves in all the right places, trapping his gaze at every turn. When his eyes returned to hers, he thought he saw a hunger there—a brief glimpse of lust he felt that must have mirrored his own.

As he snatched her bag from her hand, the warmth of her flesh brushing against his seemed to send a jolt of electricity through his fingers and up his arm. Without hesitation, he turned and headed for the stairs. "Follow me," he ordered her.

CHAPTER TWO

Who does this man think he is, bossing me around like this?

Though Gwen had found herself quietly obliging his every demand, every word he spoke in *that* tone increased her infuriation. As Blake led her inside one of the enormous guest rooms on the second story, he shut the door behind them. Placing her bag on the elegant, mahogany four-posted bed, he turned to face her. For a moment, his dark gaze seemed to study her. In the brief silence, Gwen realized just how alone they were and her indignation suddenly gave way to apprehension. What did he want from her? And why did he need them to be alone? Deep inside, she knew what she desired from him. Something she hadn't for a long time. Her thoughts dove into the passion he seemed to ignite in her and she wished for him to take her in his arms and make love to her.

"I don't think you should be here." His heavenly voice, like the caress of soft silk over skin, brought Gwen back to rational thought.

"Excuse me?" Gwen's anger returned at the realization of his statement. "I was invited."

Blake stepped toward her. Every muscle in Gwen's body locked, desperately helping her to stand her ground.

"That's exactly my point, Miss Deveraux. May I call you Gwen?"

Miffed, Gwen felt her expression harden. "Only my friends, family, and students call me Gwen. At the moment, you are none of those things to me."

Blake appeared wounded. His hand stretched out to her. "I am trying to be your friend." As his skin touched hers, his fingers gently clasping her hand, a buzz of electrical current seemed to pass between them.

Gwen wanted to pull away, but her body wouldn't let her. All she could do was hold her position, even though every nerve seemed poised to throw her into his arms or force her to run for the door. "Do you lock everyone you want to be friends with alone in a room with you?" she asked him breathily.

"We aren't locked in." He smiled.

"Good. Then I think you should go." With all her strength, Gwen snatched her hand from his and stepped away.

Blake's face became pained. "Gwen, you don't understand. I am trying to help you. My name is Blake Davenport. I'm David's brother." He took a step toward her, but Gwen flinched away. "I don't think you realize why he invited you here."

"It's Christmas, Mr. Davenport. I was invited because Emily told David that I'd be spending it alone for another year. Out of the kindness of his heart, David invited me to celebrate the holidays with them."

"Is that what he told you?" Blake's tone became indignant. "Did he also happen to mention that Emily is spending the holidays with her mother in Brisbane?"

Gwen couldn't hide her surprise. She had assumed that at least Emily, of all David's family, would be joining them for the week. "He may not have mentioned that," she told him.

Blake snatched Gwen's bag from the bed and thrust it toward her. "Then do yourself a favor and leave now. You don't know what you're really in for."

Gwen felt the shock of his words wash over her. He really meant it. He really wanted her to go. He didn't even know her. She stared deep into his eyes, willing him to change his mind. But was that a glint of fear she could see?

A knock came from behind her and the bedroom door swung open.

"Gwen. How good to see you." David's attractive face lit up with a smile as he saw her. When his gaze drifted across to Blake, his grin faltered. "Blake is showing you to your room, I see. I hope he has been behaving himself. Now, shall we?" He motioned for her to exit the room with him. "I'm sure Blake can look after your bag for you."

Torn between the two of them, Gwen chose to follow the man who wanted her to stay. Everything about Blake may have made her heart beat faster and her body quiver with anticipation, but David was the one who was genuinely interested in her and whose kindness meant that she wouldn't be celebrating Christmas alone. David deserved her trust, no matter what Blake might have told her.

CHAPTER THREE

Blake stared at the clock in the dining room, mulling over his earlier conversation with Gwen. He hadn't seen either of them since his brother had dragged her away an hour earlier. What was taking them so long? David knew dinner was at seven. If only there had been longer for them to talk in private, Blake was sure he could have made Gwen see sense. Now having met her, he was more determined than ever to protect her from his brother's plan. He thought back to when they had been alone together, her toned body with its luring curves distracting him from his task as he tried to warn her. She'd had a tempestuousness he hadn't expected, but with a sweetness and innocence that made him even more protective of her. He would never let David trick her into loving him. Blake's heart wrenched at the thought.

"I will not let that happen," he growled under his breath.

At that moment, feminine laughter echoed down the hall. David and Gwen appeared at the doorway.

David acknowledged Blake with a nod. "Prompt as always, brother."

Ignoring David, Blake couldn't take his eyes from

Gwen. Though he tried, she was careful to avoid meeting his gaze.

David's hand went to the small of her back, guiding her into the room. Gwen's genuine smile in return had Blake wishing that expression had been for him. After showing Gwen to her seat, David took his own at the head of the table, opposite Blake. Once everyone was seated, Margaret brought in their meals.

David caught Blake's attention as his dinner was placed before him. "I apologize for the choice in cuisine, Blake. I know how you loathe tofu, but Margaret was not expecting you."

Blake glanced down at his food. Tofu stir-fry. He should have known David would try anything to get him to leave them alone. Blake had always been a meat man and had never been fond of meat alternatives. Funnily enough, neither had David. His brother's antics only proved how important it was for him to keep persisting in his mission to save Gwen.

When Blake looked up, Margaret caught his eye as she left the room. Her apologetic expression said it all. He doubted she'd even known she was making the dish until Blake had confirmed his visit. It made him wonder what else he was in stall for, during his stay.

"That's quite all right, David. I'm sure tofu made by Margaret will be as marvelous as any true meat dish." Blake glanced at Gwen and their eyes met across the table.

Her expression was full of concern. "Here, Blake," she said as she stood. "We can swap meals." She carried her plate to him before he could utter a word. "It looks as though David and I have chicken, but I am quite content with tofu myself." She swapped their plates and returned to her seat.

Blake didn't know what to say. He wasn't sure if he was more annoyed by the fact that his brother had purposely deceived him with a trifling choice of dish or more impressed by the selfless nature Gwen had just displayed.

One look at David proved he felt similarly shocked. Gwen had surprised them both.

"Thank you." Blake's voice was filled with sincerity. He hoped this might mean she considered him, at the very least, a friend.

***

Having survived one of the most awkward dinners she had ever sat through, Gwen had decided to retire to her room. She knew it was early and that she may have come across to David as boring, but the tension between the brothers had been too much for her to bear any longer.

Besides, an early night will do you good, she convinced herself. Tomorrow would bring a fresh perspective and a happier atmosphere. It was Christmas day, after all.

Though she was unsure of their plans, a part of her hoped Blake might be included.

"Don't be silly," she told herself. "He's not interested in you. He's just out to ruin his brother's love life."

Even as she said it, she knew it wasn't true. Although she didn't want to believe it, there was definitely something more behind David's invitation than she'd anticipated. He'd hinted at things she wasn't ready to consider with him: whether or not she could see herself living in a place like this? If she was interested in marriage? They were all things she struggled to see the two of them doing together. But, she and Blake...those thoughts had already crossed her mind. Something about him had buried itself in her very soul. She found herself struggling *not* to think about him. He had captivated her and filled her mind with a strong desire she had never felt before. It made her wish for a perfect world, where he felt the same.

"But it's clear he doesn't, and that's that." In an effort to convince herself, her voice burst gently through the silence.

Though reality had shown it to be true, her heart ached

at the thought. Had it only been Blake who had invited her to stay. Had it only been Blake who had wanted to get to know her better. Maybe then, love would have had a real chance of blossoming.

CHAPTER FOUR

The clock radio on the bedside table glared at her with its glowing red, digital numbers. It was just before midnight. Gwen was struggling to stay asleep. The bed in the guest room was faultlessly comfortable and the house was peacefully silent. If it wasn't her surroundings disturbing her, she wondered why she was still awake. Was it Blake's cryptic warning that had her worried about David's true intentions? Or was it that Blake was sleeping in the guest room just down the hall?

Climbing out of bed, she decided to brave the dark hallway in search of a glass of water. As she closed the door quietly behind her, Gwen noticed a light on in another room. Blake had left his bedroom door ajar just enough to let the light from inside escape and paint a thick, bright line across the passageway. Creeping toward it, she peered inside.

Blake was sitting at a desk, staring at the vibrant screen of his laptop. Dressed only in black boxer shorts, the muscles in his bare back rippled as he moved. Gwen couldn't take her eyes off him. Her gaze roamed over his perfectly tanned skin, drinking in each curve of raw muscle, before settling on the soft waves of his ebony hair.

Oh, she wished she could run her fingers through that short, silky mane. Blake was truly unlike any man she had ever met before. His mere presence seemed to stir such passionate feelings inside of her, which she struggled to control. Her body yearned to be close to his. To touch him. To have his fingers caress her. The lustful thought overwhelmed her. She stumbled toward the bedroom door. As she caught herself from falling, her hand pressed against the door and it swung open.

With a start, Blake spun around.

Gwen felt a hot blush cover her cheeks. She was mortified by her behavior. "I'm so sorry. I didn't mean to interrupt." Her innocent tone relayed her dismay. "I won't bother you further."

Turning on her heel, she moved to make a quick escape. Yet before she could do so, a warm hand clasped gently around her arm. Blake pulled her to face him.

"Please, Gwen. There's no need to leave. Please stay." The deep, sensual tones of his voice pleaded with her to obey. "I was only catching up on some work, but it can wait."

"I'm so sorry, Blake." She could still feel the warm glow of her embarrassment radiating across her face. "I didn't mean to snoop. I noticed your light on. You see, I couldn't sleep, either."

Blake's smile was forgiving as he closed the door behind her. "It's fine, really." He glanced down at where he still held her arm.

Gwen's gaze followed and she was quick to free herself. Blake released her obligingly, but she couldn't help but notice that he seemed almost saddened by her reaction. As she stepped away from him, she suddenly became very aware of her appearance. Distracted by the sexy sight of him at his computer, she had completely forgotten about the fact that she was still dressed in her short, silky slip. She glanced down at herself, a new wave of embarrassment washing over her.

When her gaze rose, Blake's eyes lowered. His dark stare devoured every inch of her body with a lustful hunger. Under his intimate inspection, her nipples tingled and tightened, pressing themselves hard against the violet silk of her slip. Gwen swallowed deeply, struggling to keep her thoughts from delving into fantasy.

"What...what were you working on?" Her voice came out breathily.

Blake's gaze returned to hers. "I'll show you, if you like."

With a hand to her lower back, he guided her to the chair. She sat in his place, while he remained standing behind her. The thought of his warm, luscious body so close behind hers made it difficult for Gwen to concentrate.

"This is my latest project," he told her. Leaning in over her shoulder, he pointed to the screen.

The heavenly, masculine smell of his cologne mingling with his skin had Gwen almost entranced as she struggled to look at the images in front of her.

"I took these in France a little over a month ago." His hand slipped in front of her as he used the keyboard to jump through the images.

Gwen's whole body was tingling at his closeness. His face, mere inches from hers, had her desperate to look at him. She fought against her desire.

Focus on the photographs, she ordered herself.

As she looked through them, she could see why he had become as successful as he was. They were incredible. From the sunset seascapes to the grand waterfalls and the ancient ruins among meadows, every picture told a different story, evoked a different emotion. His talent was undeniable.

"These are amazing," she told him, her tone quietly awe-struck.

"I'm glad you like them."

She could feel his soft breath of his words on her neck.

Immediately, her thoughts returned to his close proximity. Her breathing increased.

"I should probably go." She moved to stand.

"Wait," he ordered her. His finger pointed to the screen. "It's midnight."

Confused, she turned to look at him, her lips so close to his, their noses almost touching.

"Merry Christmas." His voice dropped an octave lower as his dark eyes pierced hers.

Gwen's entire body tingled under his stare.

"Merry Christmas." Her voice escaped in a hushed whisper.

She watched as Blake's gaze dropped to her lips. Her heart beat frantically.

His warm hand cupped her cheek, his thumb caressing her skin. He inched toward her, pausing just before his lips touched hers. His eyes rose to hers, asking a silent question.

Gwen couldn't breathe. She couldn't think. Blake smelled so good. His touch on her skin was all she could focus on. She wanted him to kiss her.

Unable to control herself any longer, Gwen gave in to desire. She pressed her soft lips to his, melting at the euphoria of the embrace. Their gentle kiss soon became ardent and Blake's hands slipped down to her curvaceous behind as he lifted her off the chair. Taking a seat himself, he lowered her to straddle his lap. As her body met the warmth of his, Gwen felt the size of his erection pressing against her panties. A small moan escaped her lips as she rocked against him. His mouth left hers, leading a hot, tingling trail down her neck. Her breasts, with nipples pert, pressed into his bare chest, desperate to be touched. Blake's hands began to wander, creeping up over her thighs. His fingers slid over her skin and under her slip. As they met the top of her lace panties, they traced a delicate line. Then they slipped beneath to greet the soft, moist folds of her most erotic zone.

Gwen cried out. Reality suddenly washed over her. What was she doing? She pushed Blake away. "I can't do this."

Shock and confusion contorted Blake's expression. "Gwen? What's wrong?"

She climbed off him and straightened her slip. "This is wrong, Blake. I came here for your brother, not for you. I haven't even given David a chance." She felt so ashamed of herself, disappointed that she'd given in to her lust so easily.

"He doesn't deserve you, Gwen. Can't you see that?" Blake stood and stretched a hand out to her, but she quickly backed away. "That's what I've been trying to tell you. He doesn't want you the way *I want you*."

Gwen shook her head. "How can I trust you? I barely know you. For all I know, you're seducing me to try and keep David and me apart."

"That's not true, Gwen. You have to know that. I usually stay out of my brother's love life, but I've never felt this way before." His dark eyes appeared to be pleading with her to believe him.

She hoped he was being honest. Yet she had no proof. What did he even suspect David was planning to do to her? Lie to her? Seduce her? Wasn't she at the same risk of that from him?

"No. I have to go." Her mind and emotions a mess, she hurried toward the door. She could hear Blake's footsteps behind her. As she reached the door, he held it shut.

"Don't leave like this." He turned her to face him, trapping her between his arms. "You can trust me, Gwen. I am trying to protect you."

"Are you?" She glanced at the cage he'd made around her with his body. "It looks to me like you might be the one I need protection from." As she spat the words at him in her acid tone, she regretted them immediately.

Apparently wounded, Blake's brooding stare hardened.

"Is that what you think of me?" His voice growled with anger and menace. He released her and stepped away. "If that's how you truly feel, then leave. Since you're obviously stupid enough to believe David over me, maybe you deserve what's coming to you."

Gwen shuddered at his harsh words. Her heart felt as though he'd thrust a knife deep inside, and twisted it. She could feel her cheeks flush hot as tears welled in her eyes, blurring her vision. Desperately, she fought them back. She couldn't bear to have him see her cry.

"Fine," she choked out. "Good night, then." Though she tried to sound tough, the pain she felt was still evident in her tone. Turning away from him, she opened the door. This time, he didn't stop her. As she fled down the hall, she wished she'd never agreed to the Davenports' invitation.

***

It took every inch of muscle in Blake's body not to run after Gwen. Her accusations had wounded him, as if a hot poker burnt into his chest at each untrusting word.

How could she really think those things of me?

He was frozen at the threshold, unable to follow, unable to retreat. His hand gripped the door, contorting with the violent frustration he felt inside. He knew he should make his decision. That it was made for him. He knew she was gone and wouldn't be coming back. He prayed it was only for the night.

Blake was amazed at how quickly his desire had consumed him. From her sweet honey scent and her velvet skin to those supple curves, everything about Gwen had enticed him. His body longed to embrace hers again. To feel the soft warmth of her in his arms once more. But it was more than just sex. It was unlike anything he'd experienced before. With Gwen fitting perfectly against him in his arms, Blake had felt complete.

He had never felt that way about a woman before. Gwen was unlike all of his other flings. Sure, he might have a reputation for being a bit of a playboy, especially when he returned home from a photography expedition— though it had been years since he'd partied the way he used to. Age had caught up with him. At thirty-three, he was no longer after an easy conquest. He'd seen his friends start their own families and had begun to wish for a happiness, a contentedness like theirs. Just because David had let his marriage deteriorate and now found himself in a custody battle for Emily didn't mean that Blake's love life would end the same. No, he had to make things right. Gwen was meant for him, not for David. And she wasn't leaving this house until she knew who Blake really was and what he really wanted of her.

And that is what, exactly? he questioned himself. *A serious relationship? Love? Marriage? Children?*

He smiled at the thought. Gwen was his future. Every thought of what could be, of where he wanted to be, now involved her by his side. He had to talk to her.

Blake took a step through the door, before realizing his mistake. After her allegations had hurt him so, he had used his acid tongue to return the pain. She was furious with him now. The look in her tearful eyes as she'd left was filled with heart-wrenching pain. It would take more than a few words to win her back into his arms. Even more than a sincere *I think I love you.*

Stepping back inside his room, he finally shut the door. "Morning, then," he muttered to himself. "Come daylight, I will begin to prove to her that my feelings are true." A mix of excitement and desperation filled his being. He was about to win, or lose, the only woman he had ever begun to love.

TAMMY MANNERSLY

CHAPTER FIVE

The bright light of morning shone through the sheer, white fabric of the bedroom curtains. Still in bed, Gwen stared through them to the sky outside as her thoughts overwhelmed her. A gentle sea breeze from the open window blew the curtains up and out like fluttering angel wings. She sighed. What was she going to do? It was Christmas morning and she was the special guest of the illustrious David Davenport. And yet, all she could focus on was the events of last night. She swore she could still smell Blake on her skin. Still feel his touch on her body. He had definitely done a number on her. The charming, seductive man the magazine articles spoke of had won over her lustful body with ease. She was ashamed at how easily she'd given in to him.

"Never again," she whispered. Though she had meant it to sound determined, it had left her lips hinted with disappointment. Annoyed at her own betrayal, she sat up abruptly. "He's no good for you, honey," she told herself. "You hardly know him, and everything you do know suggests that he's just trying to get into your panties."

Though her pep talk reignited some of the anger and frustration she had felt the night before, it all dissipated with another deep sigh. Staying angry at a man who made her want to ravish him with just one look was going to be harder than she thought. Why did he have to be so devastatingly handsome? *Yes, but a handsome asshole is still an asshole*, she reminded herself. Even though she had still yet to get real proof of that. So far he'd only lost his temper with her after she had goaded him with accusations. That didn't prove he was truly horrible.

She slid out of bed with a harrumph. Why was she arguing with herself? She was here for David, after all, not his brother. Blake could do as he pleased. As long as he didn't *do* her, everything would be peachy. There was just one final problem. Did she tell David about Blake?

Gwen shook her head as she slipped on her matching violet robe. "It was a mistake," she told herself. "It won't happen again."

Besides, she wasn't about to embarrass David, or initiate an argument between the brothers, on Christmas day. No, it was better to just pretend it never happened.

Putting on a brave face and leaving the sanctuary of her room, Gwen made her way downstairs. She was determined to start the day afresh. As she reached the bottom of the stairs, Margaret appeared.

"Good morning, dear. Merry Christmas. I trust you slept well." The twinkle in Margaret's eye made Gwen blush.

"Yes. Thank you. Merry Christmas to you, too." Her voice was meek as she struggled to hide her embarrassment. Surely Margaret didn't know anything. How could she?

Taking something from her pocket, Margaret offered it to her. "Mr. Davenport asked me to pass this on. It seems he won't be available today until the party."

"Party?" Gwen was confused.

"The Davenports' famous Christmas party. The caterers and decorators will be arriving later in the day."

"Oh. I see." She frowned. Why hadn't she been made

privy to this information earlier? Perhaps David had wanted it to be a surprise? Gwen tried to hide her disappointment. She had hoped to spend a bit more time alone with David, to get to know him better.

The grey-haired housekeeper gave her a sympathetic smile. "Don't worry, dear. He was aware you may have come unprepared. There is a gift waiting for you in the library."

Relieved that the evidence of a second surprise proved the first likely the same, Gwen felt herself relax. She glanced around, trying to remember the location of the library from her tour the night before.

Noting her bewilderment, Margaret pointed her in the right direction. "Down that hall. Second door on your left."

"Thank you." Gwen's grateful sigh had Margaret stretching out a reassuring hand.

"If there's anything else you need, dear," she said. Her hand touched Gwen's. "Don't hesitate to call for me. I'm usually not too far away."

"I really appreciate that, Margaret." Gwen's face lit up with a grin. "I'm glad someone is here to help me navigate this incredible maze." Just as Gwen turned to head for the library, Margaret dropped a bombshell.

"From what I understand, the younger Mr. Davenport will be at your service for the day as well."

Gwen froze in place. David had left her to spend Christmas day alone with Blake? Surely not.

She could hear Margaret's footsteps disappearing behind her. And—was that a chuckle? She glanced over her shoulder, but the elderly housekeeper had already disappeared into the labyrinth of the mansion.

"What am I going to do?" Her pathetic question went unanswered.

Making her way down the hallway to the library, Gwen tried to ignore the apprehensive butterflies that had caged themselves in her stomach. She would be fine. She had to keep telling herself that. Her emotions were under control. It wasn't as if Blake would want to babysit her the whole day. He might not even want to see her at all, after last night. She could hope, anyway.

As she walked, she opened the folded note Margaret had given her.

Merry Christmas and my apologies, Gwen. I have been called away on an urgent work matter. To atone for my absence I hope you will accept my gift and honor me with your presence at the Christmas celebration this evening. —D

Gwen smiled to herself. Like his brother, David was capable of exceptional charm. But unlike Blake, his intentions appeared genuine. She appreciated his kind words and hoped she would get further opportunity to hear them in person at the gathering that evening.

At the library, she stepped over the threshold and took in the magnificence of the room. Antique bookshelves reached from floor to ceiling and covered every wall. Books, new, old and ancient-looking, filled each shelf in a sensibly ordered fashion. Opposite her, a lone picture window gave a tinted view of the blossoming flowers and greenery of the world outside. In the center of the room sat a thick, oak desk with hand-carved furnishings. On top, beside a detailed globe, was an elaborately wrapped rectangular box.

Curiosity led Gwen closer. She tugged at the bow and lifted the lid. At the sight of what was inside, a gasp caught in her throat.

Grasping each dainty spaghetti strap carefully, Gwen raised the stunning, full-length gown from the box. It was a dark shade of emerald with a low-cut front and an even lower-cut back. She held it up against herself, unsure if she could pull it off. As her gaze returned to the table, she noticed a pair of sparkling, silver stilettos and a jewelry case still inside. Delicately, she folded the dress and placed it next to the gift box. A second gasp of shock caught her breath at the sight of the case's glittering contents.

"I can't believe this." Her voice was full of surprise as it echoed through the silent room.

Inside was an extravagant diamond necklace with matching earrings. They were the perfect, opulent accessories to match the gorgeous gown that was probably worth more than her car.

Was David trying to make up for his desertion on Christmas morning by smothering her in lavish gifts? Probably. Did she mind? Not in the least. But if a relationship was to bloom between them, she required more of the man than his trinkets. Money and expensive presents, no matter how spectacular, could never be enough to buy her love.

After leaving the gift box in her room, Gwen asked Margaret about breakfast.

"It's being served on the back balcony," she was told.

After two wrong turns, she finally made a right and ended up outside overlooking the glistening blue water of the canal. Architecturally designed mansions lined the opposite bank, each as magnificent as the next. Many had expensive sailboats and luxury motor yachts moored beside their private jetties, while others exhibited ostentatious Jet Skis or enormous kayaks. The Davenports' mansion was no different. It had the best of both and seemed to flaunt them, like the others, in a kind of competitive fashion.

Lifting her gaze from the hypnotic sparkle of the sunlight on the canal water, Gwen took in her surroundings. The balcony, with its Grecian columns and marble floor, overlooked the tropical oasis of the Davenports' pool. Palm trees and a rock waterfall stood to the right, while red and yellow hibiscus shrubs lined the left. It was as though traveling down the few steps in front of her would lead her into an impossibly tranquil dreamscape.

Her fantasy came to life as Blake emerged from the idyllic guest house beyond the waterfall. Wearing only a tiny pair of white swim trunks, he strode over to the pool. His golden skin glowed in the warm, morning sunlight, appearing more kissable than ever. He didn't seem to notice Gwen as he dove skillfully into the crystal-clear water. He swam with talented ease along the bottom and then surfaced at the other end. When he opened his eyes, they were locked on to Gwen.

Caught staring, she felt herself blush and forced her gaze away.

"Good morning." Even his tone seemed to mock her.

"Hello." She nodded, glancing in his direction.

Blake grinned. Running his fingers through his dark mane, he slicked it back to reveal his handsome, angular features. As his hand slid down his muscular chest, Gwen couldn't take her eyes off him.

She remembered how soft his skin had felt beneath her fingertips, how rock-hard his body had been beneath hers. She craved to touch him just once more.

"I would have said 'Merry Christmas', but we've already had that pleasure." Blake's suggestive tone brought her back to reality.

Furious and mortified at the reminder, Gwen tore her gaze from his. "I thought Margaret said breakfast would be served out here."

"Oh, it has been." Blake smiled charmingly. "But I moved us into the pool house."

Gwen sighed. "Suddenly, I'm no longer hungry."

Wading to the edge, Blake hoisted himself out of the water with the strength of his perfect biceps. Droplets trickled down and dripped from his toned body as he strode over to Gwen. His golden skin shimmered in the sunlight, distracting her like a bird to mirrored glass.

"Breakfast is the most important meal of the day,

Gwen." It sounded like a command.

"I'm sure I'll survive," she snapped. But even as the words left her lips, she found herself once again distracted by his alluring physique. If he had been on the menu, she would have been starving. Yet that was exactly her problem. He probably was.

She glanced down lower until she saw something that made her whole body tingle with excitement. Blake's white trunks had become almost transparent. She knew she should look away, but the size of him seemed to captivate her. Memories from the night before, of the sensations of her body rocking against his, flooded back to her. She felt her body react and her nipples harden. Gwen licked her lips.

Blake's gaze followed hers. "Like what you see," he asked. His tone filled with a sexual promise he could surely fulfil.

Terribly embarrassed by her conspicuously lustful stare, Gwen looked skyward. "I know you're doing this on purpose," she told him. Her hands went to her hips.

"I don't know what you're talking about, love."

The humor in his tone only infuriated Gwen further. "Don't call me that. I'm nobody's 'love', and definitely not yours." Her glare in his direction was ruined with a glance downward. "Ah! Can you cover yourself, please?"

"Have breakfast with me." It was another order.

"No."

Blake shrugged. "I think I might go skinny dipping."

"Oh God, no!"

"Then have breakfast with me."

"Fine." Gwen sighed. "*If* you put some clothes on." She was cautious to keep her gaze at eye level. A private breakfast with a clothed Blake was a small price to pay when she was at real risk of ravishing him semi-nude.

"Fantastic." His triumphant tone was irritating.

Climbing a couple of steps, Blake grabbed her delicate hand in his. The surprise of his touch and the coolness of his skin had her eyes meeting his. He led her down to the pool level.

"What are you doing?"

He smiled. "Only as you asked."

"You're getting me wet."

"That's something I seem to be very good at." His deep voice was wicked.

Before she could protest, Blake spun her around in front of him. The quick motion made Gwen gasp. Casually, he slid his strong hands over her hips and held her in place, mere inches from his body.

Gwen's pulse raced and her breathing quickened at his touch. "This isn't exactly what I'd had in mind when I told you to cover up."

Blake laughed mischievously. "I'm only doing as instructed, Gwen. You never set the terms of this agreement. Now…walk." His commanding tone sent a shiver of excitement through her body.

No, ignore that!

Her thoughts and desires raged as she tried to think sensibly.

You're a strong, independent woman, capable of controlling your emotions around a rich, flirtatious playboy. No matter how handsome or charming he is. Remember, you are here for David, not for Blake.

Even as she thought it, she knew she no longer thought it true. Her heart had already fallen prey to the roguish Davenport brother. As if controlled by desire, her body obeyed Blake's instruction, and she began to walk with him to the pool house.

CHAPTER SIX

Blake escorted Gwen inside the self-contained abode opposite the pool. He had left it impeccable, besides a colorful beach towel on the bed. Complementary to the tropical theme of the pool, the furnishings gave the room a peaceful, holiday atmosphere. On the central table, circling a vibrant bouquet of exotic flowers, was the continental breakfast Margaret had arranged on silver platters.

"Wow." Gwen was clearly in awe. "This place continues to amaze me."

Reluctantly, Blake dropped his hold on Gwen's waist. "I'm glad you approve," he told her. He grabbed the towel from the bed and covered his manhood. "Help yourself to anything on the table. I'll be back in a moment." Disappearing into the en-suite, he toweled off and slipped on a spare pair of shorts. When he reappeared, Gwen was gazing outside through the French doors, croissant in hand.

She glanced back at him. Frowning, she pointed the pastry in his direction. "This isn't clothes."

"No. That's a half-eaten croissant," he teased. Her glare aroused him.

"Don't play coy," she warned him. "I know what

you're doing."

"Of course you do." He walked over to her. "We're having breakfast." He snatched the pastry from her hand and took a bite.

"Excuse me?" Her expression was full of protest.

"Would you like another?" He offered her the silver tray.

Gwen eyed him cautiously. "Am I allowed to eat this one myself?"

Blake smirked. "Of course."

Carefully, she took one and nibbled at the end.

"There's no need to look so wary." Blake couldn't hide his amusement. "We're only enjoying breakfast together."

"Is that all we're doing?" Her tone was all suspiciousness.

Blake's grin widened. "Why? Should we be doing something else?" Unable to help himself, he glanced toward the bed.

Gwen's posture tensed. "I think I should be going now."

Blake's heart lurched at the thought. His made his expression serious. "No, Gwen. I apologize. I'm only teasing, really. Please stay."

Her stern glare softened. "I'm not sure it's a good idea, Blake."

He found himself smiling as she said his name. It seemed to fill him with such a feeling of warmth that he believed he could listen to her say it all day. He couldn't let her leave like this. He had to do anything to make her stay with him.

"Would it help if I put a shirt on?"

Gwen seemed to react to the sincerity in his voice. "It would be a start."

"Done," he said. He disappeared back into the en-suite, reappearing a second later to slip on a black T-shirt. "Better?" He glanced at Gwen hopefully.

She nodded. "Much."

"Let's eat, then, and talk." Blake grabbed a silver platter and motioned to the small sitting space overlooking the pool. "I'd like to know more about this Miss Deveraux woman my niece seems so fond of."

***

Gwen bit into the last slice of pineapple. She had just told a complete stranger her whole life story. Although not unfamiliar with her physical person, Blake had been nothing to her just the day before, besides a local celebrity in the spread of a trashy magazine. It seemed odd, to her, then, that she would tell him all that made her who she was and how she came to be. The damaging effects of her previous relationship had left her lips, and so too had the passing of her parents. She expected to feel extremely vulnerable to his judgments, to his assumptions and conclusions. Yet Gwen felt content, somehow at ease and calm in Blake's presence, almost as though she welcomed his insights, his support. But how was that possible? She hardly knew him.

"I now understand why you're so guarded." Empathy filled his voice. "Trying to cope with the tragic traffic accident that took your parents from you and then having to deal with your fiancé's cheating so soon after; these life events have made you a survivor."

"I'm not sure what you mean. I wouldn't say I'm guarded." Her tone was matter-of-fact. Guarded? No. She was purposefully trying not to be.

"Even when it comes to matters of the heart?"

Gwen frowned. Being guarded against Blake wasn't wrong. Her heart was in danger with him. Besides, she was open to David. "Not when it comes to your brother. I am doing my best to be open to all possibilities."

"I see." Blake's smile was forlorn. "So you're only guarded when you're with me, then?"

Gwen's chest ached at his words. Suddenly, she felt

guilty. "I guess I feel I have to be."

"You don't trust me?"

She shrugged. "I don't trust me with you. But it's not just that. You have a…certain reputation."

"Oh, that." Blake chuckled. "Not everything in the media is true."

Gwen raised an eyebrow. Did he think he could convince her that easily?

He laughed loudly. "Okay. Not everything they gossip about me is current. My roguish image still sticks, whether I want it to or not. Every time I'm photographed with a woman, they make a fuss."

"And I'm sure there's never any reason for them to?" Sarcasm twisted her tone.

Blake smirked. "Not as much as there used to be." His words seemed to hint at an exceptional sexual prowess, as if daring her to prove him wrong.

Gwen shook her head. Damn it, he was tempting. "If I am guarded, this here—" She pointed at all of him. "This is why."

"I've no idea what you mean." His smile widened.

Her eyes rolled. "So, it must be difficult being in the spotlight all of the time."

"Smooth," he laughed. "Change the subject to avoid dealing with more serious issues."

"Oh, this is serious, Mr. Davenport." She grinned smugly. "I've told you mine, now you share yours."

"And what exactly are we sharing, Miss Deveraux?" Again, his gaze jumped to the bed.

"In your dreams," she sighed. But it was a lie. He was already in hers.

Once more, a deep, sensual chuckle of laughter filled the room. Blake's expression became more sincere as he gazed at Gwen affectionately. "Okay, love. So you want to know a little more about me?"

Sure, Gwen had read a couple of feature articles on the talented but womanizing Blake Davenport. A few, to be fair. Yet she had never found any reference to his humanitarian work, the charity he'd set up to help the homeless youth in Australia's bourgeoning cities, or his support of wildlife protection organizations, both nationally and internationally. His modesty had shone through in his apprehensiveness to discuss pastimes, alternative to his love of photography. Though once he started talking, his passion for his philanthropic work, his adoration for animals and his determination to try to make the world a better place, kept him conveying the words with such enthusiasm. She could have sworn she saw him blush at the sudden realization of his overshare.

"I apologize for going on and on," he said. He rearranged his position in the lounge chair as if he was uncomfortable. "I've no idea what you must think of me now."

She thought him some kind of wonderful, yet felt uneasy at the thought of expressing it. "Having a passion for your work, both professional and charitable, is nothing to be ashamed of, Blake."

His posture seemed to relax at her words. He smiled contentedly. "I usually find it difficult to talk about myself, especially more private matters."

Gwen returned his smile. "We have that in common," she told him. "I wonder why we felt so assured to share with each other." As she spoke, a thought came to mind. Could it be love? But that truth scared her. She was not prepared to fall in love with someone who fell so easily in lust with every attractive woman on the planet. Her heart couldn't take that strain.

Blake shrugged half-heartedly. It seemed as though he was also considering an answer. "I wonder," he said.

It was Gwen's turn to shift in her seat. All of a sudden, she felt nervous under his gaze. "I think it may be time for me to go. Breakfast is finished." She forced her smile.

"I'll see you downstairs in half an hour, then?"

His question puzzled her. "Are you going somewhere?"

Standing up, he reached a hand out to her. "*We* are going somewhere."

She allowed him to help her stand, but her expression was full of suspicion. "Do I get a say in the matter?"

Blake grinned. "No."

"Well then, do I at least get to know what to wear to this *somewhere*? What to bring?"

"Consider it a day at the beach," he told her. "As long as you bring your lovely self, I can attend to the other arrangements."

Gwen narrowed her gaze. A beach day didn't sound so bad. Noosa's Main Beach was always crowded in summer. At least then she wouldn't be at risk of more intimate time alone with Blake. Yet for some reason, she doubted he'd told her everything. A normal day at the beach? With the Davenports, it appeared as though nothing was as ordinary as it seemed.

CHAPTER SEVEN

Gwen's instincts had been right. A day at the beach, in Davenport terms, had meant a day on board their forty-eight-foot luxury yacht, motoring out of the calm waters of the canals, beyond the currents of the Noosa River and out into the turquoise of the Coral Sea. Boats of all shapes and sizes filled the river and passed the Noosa Spit, full of families making the most of their Christmas. It was a glorious day. The glow of the hot sun overhead in the vibrant blue sky reminded Gwen of why she loved Australian summers.

As they passed Main Beach, the ocean remained tranquil, much to the dismay of a few hopeful surfers sitting idly in the water on their boards. Colorful umbrellas and sun tents littered the golden, sandy beach as people, young and old, in a rainbow of swimsuits, enjoyed the sun and gentle waves close to shore. Being already after ten, the boardwalk and the restaurants that lined the foreshore were inundated with crowds.

Where Gwen sat, at the back of the flying bridge, which crowned the yacht as a third deck, she had an uninterrupted, three-sixty-degree view of Noosa's seaside charm. She was also fortunate enough, from that angle, to have an uninterrupted view of Blake's blessed form. With his back to her, he steered the massive yacht through the peaceful water as though the hull were a hot blade slicing through butter. Like Gwen, he had dressed with swimming in mind. His white cotton shirt billowed open in the breeze over his navy trunks. Thinking herself rather clever, Gwen had been strategic in her choice of outfit. Picking, over her usual bikini, a sleek, black one-piece with a white striped bodice and instead of a kaftan, a peasant blouse and jean shorts. Somehow she reasoned that the more difficult her clothing was to remove, the more likely she would survive the day without making further lustful mistakes.

Heading out of Laguna Bay, the land became more heavily treed as they passed alongside the Noosa National Park. Blake steered past the more volatile swell of the Boiling Pot waves as they crashed over the rocky cliffside and then motored the yacht into Tea Tree Bay.

"Where are you taking me?" Gwen called out, trying to be heard over the roar of the motor and the splash of the wash.

Blake glanced back at Gwen and offered her a wink. Without answering, his gaze returned to the blue ocean before them.

Rounding Dolphin Point, Blake slowed their speed as they entered Granite Bay. While they headed in slowly toward the serene coastline, Gwen took in their surroundings. The water, with its numerous hues of blue, was pristine all the way in until its waves washed gently ashore. Beyond the golden beach, grey pebbles and rocks lined the perimeter below a sheer cliff face. While the sandy shore was deserted of human life, a few hikers were making use of the walking track up high above on the cliffs, before the forest became dense.

"This is Winch Cove," Blake called out to Gwen as he slowed the yacht to a stop. "I'm heading down to drop anchor. Care to join me?" He switched the motor off and began the climb to the deck below.

Gwen followed suit, gripping the handrail as she descended the steep stairs. As she neared the bottom, Blake reached out to help her. Without thinking, she placed her hand in his. Apparently taking that as permission, Blake scooped her up, lifting her feet from the steps and pulling her close. A startled yelp left her lips as her supple body softly met the hard line of his. With their faces so close, she felt herself entranced by his dark stare. Lost in his eyes, she couldn't help but wonder if his thoughts matched the passion of her own.

Their embrace lasted only a brief moment, until her toes touched the floor. Finding the ground seemed to help her find sense. She pushed away from him.

"Thank you, but I have dismounted stairs on my own before." She had hoped to sound more grateful.

Blake's eyes widened. "On board a luxury cruiser?"

She frowned. "Well, no."

He chuckled and headed off toward the bow, leaving Gwen feeling a little sheepish.

Making her way to the stern, she basked in the startling sunlight. There was a sudden clinking of heavy chain and then a loud splash. Blake emerged from the side of the cabin.

"Looks like you're stuck here with me for a while. Unless, of course, you know how to weigh anchor."

Gwen was puzzled. "Isn't that what you just did?"

Blake's smirk proved her wrong. A pang of fear filled her with nerves as she realized she was trapped on a boat, in a secluded cove, with a man who made her want to tear his clothes off with her teeth. If only David hadn't been so lovely and Blake hadn't been such a philanderer, maybe then this situation would have filled her with opportunity, rather than dread.

"How are you at swimming?"

The sound of Blake's voice startled her. Gwen realized she was staring—at him. How lucky she was that his back was turned as he gazed out to shore.

Composing herself, she stepped next to him. "I was champion at school."

His amused expression was full of curiosity. "Really? What was your stroke?"

"Freestyle."

"You're just full of surprises," he told her affectionately.

Gwen grinned. "And you?"

He looked away, a little embarrassed. "Butterfly was my stroke at school, but I was also a surf lifesaver in my teens."

Giggling, she looked him up and down.

"What?" His voice was full of amusement.

"I'm just trying to imagine you in the little shorts and the red and yellow cap."

Blake turned to face her. His stare became suggestive. "I think I still have them somewhere. We can role-play later, if you like."

Her thoughts wandered into dangerous territory for a moment. Blake—shirt off—slow-motion running down Main Beach to rescue her. She blinked the fantasy away. He had to be teasing her, but it was difficult to tell if he was really kidding.

"What were we talking about? That's right. Swimming." She gazed out over the water at the golden beach before them. It had to be no more than a few hundred meters away. Moving around him, she stepped to the deck's edge. "Race you?"

A hand went to Blake's chest as he feigned adoration. "A woman after my own heart."

She rolled her eyes. Without giving a second thought to the fact that her cleverly arranged attire would be abandoning her, Gwen began to undress. Having stripped off her shirt, she took off her shorts, tossing both on a seat nearby. Blake followed her lead, undoing the few buttons keeping his shirt on and then throwing it on top of her clothes.

"Shall we?" He seemed too keen.

"Wait," she told him, stretching an arm in front of his chest to keep him from jumping. "On your marks." Gwen felt an invigorating rush of anticipation as she spoke.

"Get set." Blake's tone seemed to match hers, full of humor and excitement.

"Go!" Gwen yelled as she dived in. She was sure she heard a protest to her cheating as she glided through the air.

Slicing through the calm ocean with minimal splash, she swam under water for a few strokes before resurfacing. The cool, salty water was refreshing after the heat of the bright summer sun and she relished the exhilaration of the race. Without a glance at Blake, she began to swim effortlessly to shore.

***

Blake couldn't be sure if he had let Gwen win or if she was even better than he'd expected. Her cheating had been lucky to give her a few seconds head start and, under normal circumstances, he would have easily recovered that ground over a few hundred meters. Yet, she'd beat him. He was astounded by her. Everything about her seemed to surprise and captivate him. He could only hope she felt the same in return.

As he climbed to his feet, wading through the shallows, he stared at her sexy figure on the sand. "You cheated," he called out to her.

She giggled. "Did I? How terribly rude of me. Shall I give you a head start next time?" Her laugh was infectious.

"My, Miss Deveraux, how cheeky you are! Do you behave this way in front of your students, too?" Blake couldn't hide the joviality from his voice.

Her grin widened. "Who do you think I learned this from?"

Blake's bare feet reached the warm sand as he strode toward her. "Well then, I think some discipline is in order. What's the punishment for cheating these days?"

Gwen shrugged. Her expression became all innocence and false ignorance as she held her ground.

Blake smirked. "A spanking it is, then," he told her.

Her eyes widened as he lunged for her playfully. An adorable squeal of laughter escaped her lips as she ran from him. Blake followed in hot pursuit, loving the literal chase even more than he'd once enjoyed the figurative one.

Gwen zigzagged up and down the beach in her attempt to escape him, giggling every time she spotted him close behind. "You can't catch me," she teased him.

Oh, but he could. Watching her feminine curves bounce as she ran seemed to spur him on. There wasn't much he wouldn't do to be able to caress her body beneath his. His whole being seemed to crave her.

Suddenly, Gwen slowed. She had cornered herself at the end of the beach between the cliff-face and a large boulder. Her only way out was the ocean. She turned to face him, arms raised in defeat.

"Okay, truce," she pleaded with a smile.

Blake stopped barely a meter from her. He narrowed his gaze as though considering his options. "Very well." He nodded and reached out as if to shake on their agreement.

Gwen's posture seemed to relax, and she chuckled. "You had me worried there, for a moment." She put her hand in his.

Blake took advantage of her mistake and pulled her to him. Spinning her around as she gasped, he slipped a leg behind her knee. As she lost balance, he cradled her softly to the sand. With his wet body above hers, separated by mere inches, he stared into her green eyes.

"New punishment." His voice deepened. Blake couldn't help himself. Gwen was once again in his arms and he wasn't about to squander another opportunity.

**

Gwen swallowed nervously. Her body yearned for Blake to touch her. Every cool water droplet that trickled from his body to hers felt electrified, sending tingling sensations to sensitive regions she wished his hands would explore. But his tone had her concerned. It was difficult enough to spend time alone with him without making a mistake, but in his embrace, she knew she wouldn't be able to control her desire.

"W-what did you have in mind?" Her voice was shaky and timid.

Blake grinned roguishly. "A kiss."

Her breath caught in her throat. She had to say no. It wasn't right. What about David?

What about Blake?

Her thoughts were torn, her expression no doubt timid and frozen while her mind battled an internal war.

"Blake, I-I can't." She touched her palm to his chest, hoping to push him away.

As if acting on instinct, he snatched it and lowered her arm above her head. He was quick to do the same to the other. His fingers intertwined with hers as he held her hands in place.

Gwen had never felt so vulnerable, yet so aroused. She felt her pulse quicken in expectation. Every nerve felt as if it were longing for his body to touch hers. She could barely breathe.

His lips hovered above hers. His dark eyes searched her soul. "Only one word will stop me." His voice was a whisper.

Gwen knew the word: *no*. Yet she couldn't say it. She didn't want to. In that moment, all she wanted was Blake.

A satisfied smile crossed his lips. His head bent down. Lightly, his mouth brushed over hers.

Gwen felt her nipples tighten at his touch, sending a quiver of pleasure even lower. His gentleness only seemed to enhance her sensitivity. She wanted more. Unable to control herself any longer, her lips captured his.

Responding to her lust, Blake kissed her hungrily. His hard body dropped to meet the line of hers. As the weight of his erection found a home between her thighs, a soft moan escaped Gwen's lips. The feeling of his body melding with hers was almost an unbearable ecstasy. At her encouragement, Blake pressed harder against her until her legs wrapped demandingly around his. Only their swimwear prevented them from absolute bliss.

Their kiss became voracious. Blake's teeth nipped at Gwen's lower lip in a pleasurable play of dominance. She felt utterly entranced. Rational thought had left her. Blake was all she could think about. How he kissed her, how he touched her, how she wanted him inside her.

She was tugging at his swim trunks when she heard the laughter. Blake broke their kiss and glanced up. She followed his gaze. High up on the cliff, on the walking trail, were two adolescent boys. They were pointing down at the lustful couple and laughing. The sound was barely audible over the gentle wash of the waves curling over the shore.

Still holding Gwen close, Blake glanced back down at her. He smirked. Gwen couldn't help but mirror his expression. She felt like a teenager again, where hormones and desire overrode sense. It was a joyous emotion, a freeing feeling. She felt surprisingly naughty, having behaved in such a desirous fashion. A cheeky giggle burst from her lips and Blake was quick to join her. They laughed loudly together. Gwen hadn't felt so alive in years.

All of a sudden, to her awful disappointment, Blake freed her from his embrace and climbed to his feet. He stretched out a helpful hand to her. His grin was so contented.

"Perhaps it's time for another swim," he told her.

Once again rejecting her disloyal emotions and her desperate longing for him, Gwen let Blake help her to her feet. She hid her feelings with a provocative smile. "You want to get beaten again, so soon?"

He chuckled, still holding her hand. "No. I thought it the best option to get rid of all the sand."

He motioned to his body and then to hers. Both were covered in a film of golden crystals.

"Alternatively, I can offer to brush you down myself." He wiggled his free fingers at her playfully.

Gwen considered it for a moment. While she would have let him grope every curve of her body only moments before, their interruption had brought back some common sense.

She giggled at him and snatched back her hand from his. "I don't think so. You can keep your spirited fingers to yourself." With a coquettish grin, she ran off toward the water.

CHAPTER EIGHT

Blake watched Gwen intently from where he sat opposite her at the dining nook. They were safely back aboard the yacht and enjoying the picnic lunch Margaret had prepared for them.

Upon returning to the luxury cruiser, Blake had made a point of winning their swimming race. He had wanted to prove to Gwen that he rarely lost and, for that matter, that he was a man worthy of someone as exquisite as her. Although not usually competitive, especially with the female of the species, winning had definitely fulfilled some primal instinct in him. And he was sure that Gwen had been impressed.

As that thought crossed his mind, her dazzling green eyes met his. She smiled at him, curiously.

"Do I want to know what you're thinking?" It was a question asked as if hopeful, rather than just to get a reply.

Blake felt himself grin stupidly. Her presence seemed to fill him with such elation that he found it almost impossible not to be happy around her. Not wanting to give his precious thoughts away, he decided to inquire about something he'd long been wanting to know the honest answer to.

"Why did you agree to David's invitation?" He made his tone inquisitive, but kind and non-judgmental. He hoped she wouldn't find it intrusive.

Gwen's gaze left his and her lips pursed as she considered her response. "I realize it may have seemed strange, because I hardly know your brother." With a nervous expression, she glanced at him momentarily, as if assessing his reaction. "I guess I didn't know what I was hoping to achieve by agreeing. I just felt like it was time to move on, beyond the heartbreak and painful loss of my parents." Gwen sighed and stared down at her hands. "I just didn't want to be afraid anymore."

"When David asked me to join him for the holidays, I saw an opportunity for me to begin saying yes, to start being brave again." Her gorgeous green eyes met Blake's once more. "When he asked me so suddenly and so charmingly, I began to think there was still hope for me to be happy. It helped me believe that maybe, after all I'd been through, someone could still love me."

Her sad, sincere words tugged at Blake's heart. How could someone as kind, compassionate, intelligent, and genuine as Gwen believe she was in any way difficult to love? He had known her less than twenty-four hours and already felt besotted with her. She was the most incredible woman he'd ever met. Not to mention the most radiantly beautiful, though she underrated that as much as she'd undervalued her captivating personality and lovability. Had she never been told how stunning she was? How caring and considerate? Blake shook his head at her.

"How could you ever question that?" He held her hands in his, caressing them reassuringly.

Gwen shrugged. She couldn't meet his eyes. Her cheeks had become rosy and her eyes glistened as if she was fighting off tears.

"You are an amazing woman, Gwen. Any man would be blessed merely to know you. Are you so unaware of your own uniqueness, your exquisiteness? Surely, you must find yourself surrounded by men professing their love to you?"

She glanced up at him, tears welling in her eyes. Her expression was full of incredulity and innocence. "I appreciate the kind words, Blake, but I'm a realist. I know I'm nothing special." Her voice was pained as it escaped her lips.

Blake couldn't believe what he was hearing. *Nothing special?* In less than a day, she had become the most special thing to him, the most important thing in the world to him. He held her hands tighter. He had to tell her how he truly felt.

"You've no idea how mistaken you are, love. In seeing you, I was enthralled. In meeting you, I was enlightened. In knowing you, I *am* enamored. You are everything you deny, and more. Now that I know you exist, I have been ruined for a life without you in it."

***

Gwen's heart skipped a beat at Blake's words. For a moment, she forgot how to breathe. He couldn't really mean what he'd said. *Could he?* Though they had shared truths she'd kept from even her closest of friends, they were still—in many meanings of the word—strangers. A full day had not yet passed since their first meeting, and while their chemistry and lust for each other was obvious, Gwen had a difficult enough time trusting her own heart's professions of infatuation, than believing his. No, it couldn't be true. Surely this was just part of his charm, part of his plan to bed her, win her over before his brother. Could a renowned playboy ever be so sincere about love?

Gwen breathed in deeply. "You're a real charmer, you know that?" She pulled her hands free of his. She hadn't meant her words to sting, but they had come out sharp.

Blake's brow furrowed at her physical rejection of him. "I wasn't trying to be charming," he told her.

Gwen had never heard him more sincere. Yet how could she believe him? His reputation proceeded him, and not in a good way. How could she trust her heart around a man who was skilled at breaking them?

She shook her head at him and stood up from the table. "How can I be sure you mean those things?" Her tone was less accusatory, more matter-of-fact. "Everything I know about you suggests otherwise. I can't even trust my instincts around you: you are that good, that charismatic. I don't even have proof that you're capable of the kind of love and admiration you speak of."

Blake left the table and followed her across the room. Gwen began to pace, as though trying to process the situation.

"You're overthinking this, love. This is new to me, too. I'm not one to experience emotions like this every day. Something in me has changed since I met you." He placed a light hand on her shoulder, but she shrugged it off.

Her gaze searched his and she frowned.

"Would you question my motives so harshly if we'd met under different circumstances?" Blake's tone was calm, rationalizing.

Gwen sighed, wearily. "Maybe not so harshly." Was she really being so unreasonably critical of his romantic pursuit of her?

Blake grabbed her shoulders gently, keeping her in place. "Then why are you judging me so? As you like to remind me, we are still strangers in many ways. Don't you want to take the opportunity to get to know me, the real me, before you make up your mind and dismiss me forever?"

Gwen bit her lower lip in thought. The pain seemed to help her see sense. It was unlike her to condemn someone purely on reputation. Even their sweet and sexy interludes had not been exactly as overwhelmingly seductive on his part as she had expected. On each occasion, she had been just as in the lustful moment as he had and so, was equally to blame for the inappropriate behavior. He had yet to seduce her into something she did not want to do. Perhaps he was more of a gentleman than his media-created character suggested?

Gwen grabbed his hands from her shoulders and held them in hers. "Of course I do." Her tone was full of compassion and sincerity. "I want to know you better. You have already become so important to me, too. I feel as though we can talk about anything, like we can connect on a deeper level, as though we have known each other for years."

Pausing, Gwen swallowed deeply. She was struggling to say what she had to. For some reason, her heart ached at the thought of labelling their blossoming relationship in the form that was necessary. Every fiber of her being wanted to be more than just *friends* with Blake, but she couldn't do that to David—or bear the risk to herself.

"I feel the same way," Blake told her. A smile crossed his lips.

"I'm glad." Gwen's smile in return was pained. "But I want to get to know you as a friend. Only as a friend."

Blake frowned. His eyes darkened with hurt. "I know you feel it, too. This spark between us."

He snatched a hand free from hers and caressed her face gently. Instinctively, she leaned in to his touch.

"Gwen, these kinds of feelings don't ignite often. People spend their whole lives seeking the chemistry that sparks between us so naturally."

Gwen bit her lip as she pulled away from him. "But it's not right," she told him. "In the same way it applies to you, I owe it to David to get to know him better before I make my decision. His feelings are just as important as ours and, without his desire to get to know *me* better, I wouldn't even be here now. I owe it to him to see if our relationship could blossom into more."

Blake's eyes narrowed angrily. "You don't owe him anything, love. You shouldn't fear for his feelings when it's yours you should be most concerned with. He's a big boy, he can cope. But you—you still don't really know the true reason you're here. You shouldn't trust him so easily."

In the light of Blake's misdirected anger, Gwen became infuriated. "I know what your brother told me. I know why David invited me here and until I know differently, I am willing to give him the benefit of the doubt."

Blake's dark gaze glared down at her. "How can you be willing to trust him so easily and yet you constantly challenge my motives?"

"I have never heard a negative word about him," Gwen growled. "But stories of your mischief regularly inundate the media. So much so, in fact, that even if what you say is true—that their stories are falsified or based on past events—there are still too many in circulation to believe that all have been developed to shame you and seek ratings. Surely, some must still be based on fact. David, on the other hand, is rarely publicized and when he is, the theme is always positive."

"That's because he pays off those who wish to publish bad press and I couldn't care less about what the masses think of me or my personal life." Blake's voice was deepened by rage.

Gwen felt her jaw drop. Was Blake really speaking the truth? Was the only reason the brothers' reputations differed due to the fact that one was willing to bribe the media industry, while the other found it easier to let them scramble for false gossip? During their chat earlier that morning, Blake had revealed a number of philanthropic tendencies and charitable pursuits, none of which had ever been broadcast to the public. Perhaps he was being honest with her? Perhaps David was only ever portrayed in such a positive light because of his associations with the mass media? It did make sense, but what proof did she have besides Blake's word? And she was still yet to decide how much that was worth.

Stepping close to him, Gwen put a calming palm to his

bare chest. She gazed into his dark eyes. They still glowered at the insult and indignity his character had suffered.

"I want to believe you, Blake." She made her voice soft, her words reassuring. "When I look at you, I feel as though I see the truth: you are raw with honesty, completely at ease with your own personality. It is both refreshing and terrifying to be around someone so confident and certain of themselves and what they want."

Blake's hands held hers affectionately against his chest. His expression softened and a small smile appeared.

"But," Gwen said the word warily, "I still don't know you well enough to be sure that this persona, this man I've grown so fond of, is in fact a reality and not some concoction created to try to interfere with your brother's future happiness."

Blake's gaze narrowed and the defiant anger in his eyes that had dissipated a moment earlier, flickered back to life. He opened his mouth to speak, but before he could defend himself, she interjected.

"Please, Blake." She slipped her hands from his grip and cupped his face tenderly. "Understand that I am not saying that you are not everything I want to be true and more. I believe you have my best interests at heart and I feel as though you truly care for me, as I do for you. But at the moment, that is not enough. I feel obliged to give David the chance he deserves and no harsh words from you will sway me in wanting to create my own opinion of him."

Glancing away from him momentarily, Gwen sighed deeply. When her gaze returned to his, her expression had grown saddened.

"I don't know what there is between us," she told him. "But right now I can't give you anything more than friendship. I need that to be enough."

Blake's expression was forlorn as he digested her words, but it took only a moment for his gaze to return to a defiant state.

"And if I say no? If I say I don't care and I won't agree to any of this? What then?"

Gwen found herself gobsmacked. She didn't have an answer to any of his questions. She believed she had been more than reasonable with her honest and insightful explanation of why any romance between them should cease. She had hoped he would recognize the difficulty of her plight and understand her reasons for hesitation. She felt as though he would see her request as she did: as a necessary complication that would inevitably decide their future for them. Never in any scenario had she thought that he would fight her on it. But she had miscalculated one thing—in the short time she'd known him, Blake had never been reasonable.

"I am waiting for an answer, Miss Deveraux."

Her hands slipped from his face, but he grabbed them before they fell.

"Lost for words, are we?"

Under his challenging stare, all her prior bravado had left her. She nodded. "I can't believe you're serious?"

"And why not? Why should I not take the opportunity to fight for you when you are so quick and willing to offer yourself to my morally bankrupt brother? What kind of gentleman would I be just to sit back and watch you sacrifice yourself to the wicked wolf? No, Gwen, I won't accept your friend request. I choose to throw my hat in the ring. I am not one to back away from a challenge, especially not one I know I can win."

With that, Blake dragged her into his strong arms, trapping her against the hard, bare muscles of his chest. His lips covered hers in a possessive and passionate kiss. Instinctively, Gwen melted into his arms, but soon, sense returned. She broke their embrace and pushed free of him. His smirk in return was both triumphant and charming.

Gwen panted heavily, breathless with a heady mixture of lust and fury. She glared at him, assessing him from a safe distance. "You, sir," she told him as she fought to catch her breath, "are the wolf. And it's *you* I'll have to learn to keep my distance from."

Blake's laughter in response only incited her anger.

"I'd like to see you try," he told her.

CHAPTER NINE

As the luxury cruiser docked at the Davenport mansion's pontoon, Gwen was quick to make her escape. She didn't want to be confined to close quarters with Blake any longer. Yet her instinct of flight was not caused by the incessant attempts of seduction that she had expected from Blake, but by her own desire to be close to him, to touch him and have him touch her. In fact, after their dramatic discussion, Blake had become more than amicable and had made an obvious point of keeping his distance. He seemed to restrict conversation to simple topics; his photography and her teaching had been the primary focuses. He had even intentionally found a reason to move away from her whenever she would near.

It was driving her crazy! For some reason, the distance he was deliberately putting between them only made her want to be closer to him, to have him talk to her with the same passion and emotion his voice had been full of earlier. She wanted him to hold her, to kiss her. And even worse, she wanted him to want her as much as she seemed to want him. The tension was unbearable and inextinguishable. At one point, she'd even felt as though she had been chasing him around the room. And yet, he appeared to barely notice her struggle. Whether he had just been playing coy, pretending to be innocent to her obvious lust for him, or whether he truly was oblivious, either way, she couldn't handle another moment of it.

As Gwen hurried up the jetty toward the gate and the sanctuary of the shore, she could hear Blake calling out to her. Along the way she passed two men in matching uniforms carrying a box of colored lights. They smiled as they neared and she noticed their shirts bore the logo of renowned local party planner, Best Events. Clearly, preparations for the night's Christmas party were well underway. She nodded a silent greeting and hurried on by. She didn't want to give them the chance to stop her or slow her down, giving Blake an advantage to catch up.

Slipping through the barrier to the exotic, Bali-inspired terrace, Gwen didn't wait to hear the gate close behind her. In fact, she thought to herself as she climbed the steps to the poolside garden beyond, had it even closed? As she went to glance over her shoulder, she had the sudden realization that she wasn't alone.

"How did you get here so fast?" Her tone was snippy and she regretted it immediately. It wasn't all his fault she was so frustrated. She didn't stop to hear him out, but continued to hurry toward the main house.

Blake grinned at her, keeping her pace. "My, my, love, if I didn't know better, I'd say you were trying to get away from me."

Her chuckle in reply was embarrassingly anxious. She cut it short as soon as she realized that she was emitting such a humiliating sound.

Blake laughed.

Gwen was certain it was at her, not with. She sighed. "I have to start getting ready."

Blake's expression became puzzled. "We arrived back early. It's not even four."

She shrugged. "I have to strip down and shower, then try to squeeze into the dress your brother gave me. I've never been to a prestigious party like this before and I definitely don't want to have a wardrobe malfunction."

Snatching her hand, Blake forced her to stop running from him. It was the first time he'd touched her since his vow to win her over. It sent a jolt of electrical current up her arm and through her body, making even the most sensitive of areas tingle with anticipation. Her conscience chided her at the reaction. *For God's sake, it's only my hand.*

"I'd be happy to help in any way I can, especially with the first part." Blake's tone had returned to being suggestive. It was almost a relief to hear him flirt.

She looked up at him, hoping her eyes didn't betray her, even though it felt like they were pleading for him to let her go. "I'm sure I'm quite capable of doing all those things by myself." She managed a small smile.

For some reason, she could handle their playful behavior. It was much better than feeling as though her desire for him was one-sided. Something about his touch, though, had changed. She seemed to seek it more, to crave it even more than before. It was a constant fight for her to stop herself from walking into his arms. Maybe it was because he had kept it from her for what had felt like so long? Or maybe it was due to the fact that they had both admitted their intimate feelings for each other just hours before? Whatever it was, the feeling of his fingers on her skin felt more intoxicating than ever. It was all she could do not to sneak that hand down the front of her shorts.

She shut her eyes tight at the thought. How could she think such a thing? She was about to be David's companion to the most illustrious function she'd ever attended. She couldn't entertain thoughts of his brother pleasuring her, at her own instruction. Gwen was mortified by her desires.

***

Blake watched Gwen carefully. Her face was flushed

and her lovely eyes were focused on the ground. He would pay any amount of money to know what she was thinking.

Though it had been a struggle, he'd given her space for most of the afternoon, after realizing that he could push her away by being too interested, too forceful. And that was something he definitely didn't want to do. It was only now, at the thought they were about to be separated, that he found himself reverting back to his mischievous behavior. He didn't want her to disappear inside, into David's arms, without first being reminded of his feelings for her.

With his free hand, he stroked her cheek dotingly. She seemed to shiver beneath his touch. He cupped her jaw and gently raised her face, so that her eyes would meet his. She looked almost afraid.

"Are you okay, love?" His voice was deep with genuine concern.

She bit her lip as she gazed into his eyes. Eventually she nodded. "I should go."

He frowned resignedly. "If you feel you have to."

With what seemed like almost every ounce of strength she had, Gwen took a single step back from him. His fingers fell from her face and he released his hold on her hand.

Fear struck Blake's heart like a sharp blade. Had he already pushed her too far? Did she no longer want anything to do with him? The thought was suffocating. He opened his mouth to question her, to beg forgiveness and plead with her to stay. But before he could form the words, he thought better of it. Perhaps she just needed space. They had shared a great deal together that day: feelings, desires and love. It made sense that she might require some time to process, even if he didn't.

Blake forced a small smile. "I'll see you in a couple of hours, then." He tried hard not to pose it as a question. She clearly didn't need his over-eagerness interfering with her review of the day's events.

Without another touch, even forming fists to avoid his hands wandering inappropriately, Blake moved away. As he walked around the pool toward the stairs leading to the balcony and main house beyond, he fought with himself not to look back at her. Treading the last few meters to the rear entry was an agonizing eternity filled with incredulous feelings of uncertainty. Of course he would see Gwen again. Yet without that final glance, he found himself overwhelmed with dread. Just the thought of never again having the pleasure of gazing at her beautiful face, being in the presence of her unique and vibrant personality, scared the hell out of him. Finding strength in his trepidation, Blake vowed that if there was one final thing he could accomplish in his lifetime, it would be to make Gwen his to love, honor, and cherish.

From where he stood, assessing his reflection in the mirror of the mahogany vanity, Blake glanced over at the clock on his bedside table. It was almost seven. The guests would be arriving shortly. Returning his attention to knotting his black tie, he tried to ignore the anger welling up inside him.

After he had left Gwen by the pool garden, hours before, he'd run across David. Innocent as he could sometimes be to the severe extent of his older brother's schemes, Blake had thought it best to try to be honest with him. He'd been stupid enough to believe that once he'd given David some understanding of how he felt for Gwen, and how she returned his feelings, that his brother would relinquish all desire to seek her for his depraved requirements. But that belief had been based on his brother having morals and concealing a heart, both of which, it seemed, Blake had misjudged him on.

In fact, David had been so put out by Blake's confession that he had warned him to stay clear of things that didn't concern him and had threatened to move up the schedule of his plans. It was as though Blake had interfered with the arranging of a business deal, not the wooing of a wonderful woman. Moving his only pawn, Blake had tried to sway David, with the risk of Gwen discovering the debauched truth behind his brother's invitation. But in response, David had just laughed in his face. He seemed to think that the mere fact Blake had yet to share that information with her, meant that he never would. As though something deep within Blake's conscience would not let him betray his brother in such a way.

Although Blake had scoffed and pledged to prove otherwise, the fury flourishing within him was partly due to the fact he knew his brother was right. While he wished to protect Gwen in every way possible, he was struggling deeply with the decision of whether to break the bond of brotherhood at the risk of losing it forever. Why couldn't David just come clean? Surely he could find another woman to take Gwen's place in his scheme? He didn't require her in particular, did he?

"No." Blake shook his head as he glared at himself in the mirror.

Gwen may have been an incredibly special woman, but as just a random choice for an unloving, unappreciated marriage? No, her role could easily be filled by numerous others. David had no right to single her out and coerce her into such a difficult predicament and unhappy arrangement.

With his tie complete, he slipped on his jacket and evaluated his reflection. Externally, he was the black-tie perfection that was to be expected at the elitist occasion he was about to attend. But internally, he was a smoldering mixture of rage and self-loathing. He had to tell Gwen the truth about David as soon as possible. A crisis of conscience was nothing when he faced an existence without Gwen, or a life with her miserably married to his unscrupulous brother.

"Screw David" Blake spat out the words. "I'll tell her tonight." Feeling stronger with the resolution, his posture straightened.

As if in response, the triumphant chimes of the doorbell echoed throughout the house. David's famous Christmas party was just about to begin. Though Blake was apprehensive of what the evening would hold, he felt certain revealing the truth to the woman he loved would set them both free.

CHAPTER TEN

Gwen paced the length of her room. This was not due to the fact she had some seriously intoxicated butterflies, fluttering around drunkenly in her gut—though she had those as well—but because she was still learning to walk in the extravagant silver stilettos David had procured for her.

As she was so naturally tall herself, wearing high heels was more of a rare occurrence for her and so, left her with a little vertigo. When the last of her wobbliness had been incorporated into a strategic hip wiggle, Gwen stopped in front of the full-length mirror. She couldn't help but stare at herself. She had never seen her figure presented in such a snug, sensual garment, or with such exceptionally enhanced feminine curves. The dark emerald gown left nothing to the imagination, revealing her braless cleavage in front and bare skin down to her hips at the back. She was relieved that her lace panties remained hidden just below, but had to wonder whether David had been hoping the dress design might hint at her wearing no underwear at all.

Yeah, as if that was going to happen. She smiled at herself in the mirror. No knickers would have left her in a dangerous territory, and not just at the risk of Blake or possibly

David's advances, but at the mercy of her own wicked desires.

Gwen assessed herself in the mirror. Her long, auburn hair was twirled into an elegant bun, with only a few wisps left free to soften her angular cheekbones. An hour earlier, Margaret had introduced her to a hairdresser and makeup artist named Natalia, who had been organized by David to doll her up for the evening. Though she had asked Natalia for a more natural look, it seemed David had already prearranged that as well. Natalia had told her there was no room for natural at this sort of party and had proceeded to highlight her features with more makeup than Gwen had ever worn in her life.

Starring at her reflection, with her dark smoky eyes and blood red lips, Gwen recognized someone passably model-esque staring back. She had to admit Natalia had done an excellent job in turning her quite ordinary appearance into the extraordinary. And she'd been even more grateful for the effort when she donned the opulent diamond necklace and matching earrings. Without the cosmetic enhancement, her features would have been hidden beneath the glittering sparkle of her accessories. Taking in her full appearance, she noted her similarities to the women in the trashy magazines she loved to read. Dressed as she was, she could have been heading anywhere the elite were known to frequent: an awards ceremony, a movie premiere, even a royal wedding.

At the thought, the pressure seemed to mount and Gwen reminded herself to breathe deeply. She was brutally aware of how much she didn't belong in the world she was about to dive into. Just because her appearance would now allow her to sneak through the celebrated crowd, didn't mean she could so easily fit in. She knew who she really was, just an average primary school teacher thrust into the world of the wealthy and the beautiful. She probably wouldn't know anyone at this event, besides those she recognized from the media. In fact, she didn't even know of anyone who might be attending. David and Blake were yet to inform her. The drunken butterflies that had quietened in her gut returned to their rambunctious behavior.

How could she possibly survive the evening? Surely David, as host, would have no time to share with her. But then how could she keep her distance from Blake, when she knew no one with whom to make small talk?

Gwen drank the glass of champagne Margaret had left for her. Her nerves made her pray for the drinks to keep flowing. Perhaps then she could retire early, from tiredness, and escape the potential dramas the night could hold. She glared over at her reflection.

"You will stay away from Blake," she ordered herself. She wished there had been more certainty in her voice.

Though they had shared many intimate encounters, both physical and emotional, Blake's behavior that afternoon had put further doubt into her mind about the truth of his feelings for her. How could he have left her standing there without a second glance? She knew it was wrong of her to wish for such a thing, when she had been so adamant with him about her very practical hope to be friends and no more. But her heart had longed for him to suffer at his leaving her as much as she had suffered at seeing him leave. Maybe then she could believe wholeheartedly that what he'd said he felt for her was real?

Yet her mind filled with anxiety at the thought. Short of him doing something so profoundly obvious and reckless like...*proposing*, she would continue to question his sincerity. Yes, the mere absurdity of proposing to a near stranger would likely convince her of his heart's true desire.

Gwen laughed at herself. The extravagantly dressed model in the mirror laughed with her.

Clearly, she was in over her head and couldn't be saved. She was in love with one brother, who probably didn't love her, and indifferent to another, who possibly did.

"Oh, tonight is going to be lots of fun." The sarcasm in her voice told the empty room otherwise.

***

Blake had reached the bottom of the stairs in the entry. The doorbell had just rung again and he had offered to get it, sending Margaret away to continue to oversee the caterers in the kitchen. As he quickened his pace to the grand front door, he wondered where his brother was lurking. Hopefully David, being the showman that he was, would remain in clear sight for the whole evening, entertaining his guests and leaving Gwen safely unattended. That would give Blake the opportunity he needed to confess to Gwen the truth of her situation, revealing the duplicitous scheme his brother had lured her in for. It was a task he wished he was not obligated to undertake, but he could no longer be an accomplice just to ensure the love of his own brother. Gwen needed to know the truth.

Blake opened the door and greeted their guests. It was another elderly billionaire with another surgically optimized beauty queen on his arm. After a formal welcome, he directed them through to the enormous recreation room at the back of the mansion. He had to admire the ostentatious decorations David had arranged.

A trio on piano, cello, and violin played Christmas carols in a classical fashion while wait staff served drinks and canapés to the growing crowd. In the far corner, looming over the guests in a glistering mass, was a giant Christmas tree, complete with all the trimmings, including professionally wrapped faux presents at its base. Beyond the commotion, folding French doors opened entirely to overlook the brightly lit pool and its exotic landscaping. Every corner of the grounds outside was illuminated with thousands of white and colored fairy lights, giving the mansion's gardens a magical ambiance. Even the luxury cruiser had been adorned with enough twinkling bulbs to turn it into a floating spectacle. Blake couldn't deny his brother's ability to organize a great celebration, no matter the expense.

Leaving the newest guests to mingle, Blake headed back to the entry. Unlike the rowdy, reckless person he used to be, he was relieved to have the opportunity to be alone once more. The thought made him marvel at the fact that he used to find these events effortless and amusing, usually viewing them as an opportunity to bed the next hottest woman in television. It was amazing how quickly things could change. It had only been a few years since he'd lived for the party lifestyle. But reaching thirty had been a pivotal point, forcing him to re-evaluate his life and ambitions, giving him a deeper perspective of what he wanted. With the changes he'd pledged to make, he had achieved far greater success in his career than he imagined, realizing a potential and natural talent that he had only ever utilized briefly in the past. Yet while his photography fame had increased, his romantic pursuits dwindled. He had discovered that he wanted to find a partner, rather than continue to add to his long list of one-night stands. But for three more long years, he'd struggled to find someone whose feelings he returned.

He stared at the lavish, dark oak double doors before him. He smiled at the memory of Gwen stepping over that threshold, all anxious and innocent as she'd entered, her soft curves trapped in her short, paisley dress. He couldn't believe it had been only yesterday. She was enough to have him believe in love at first sight.

The light tap of heels on the marble stairs tore Blake from his thoughts. Turning to face the sound, he saw a tall, red-haired nymph frozen halfway down the staircase. An elegant hand gripped the banister tightly, while her vibrant green eyes stared down into his.

"Evening." Her gentle voice caressed his ears.

Blake's gaze drank in the tantalizing sight of her curvy

figure barely covered by the emerald green silk of her gown. Oh, how he longed to touch her again, to feel the warmth of her soft body pressed against him. The mere thought sent blood rushing southward, forcing him to fight quickly to control his hardening erection.

Blake released a breath he hadn't realized he was holding. "Evening, love."

Gwen frowned at him. It only made his stupid grin widen.

Ignoring his delight, she continued carefully down the steps until she reached the floor. Keeping her distance from him, she glanced up warily.

"I thought you would already be in there." She tilted her head toward the hallway through which the sounds of guests' chatter and laughter echoed.

Blake shook his head. "Why would I be in there when *you* are still out here?" His playful tone was filled with more sincerity than he'd expected to hear.

Gwen's expression became puzzled. "You sound as though you mean that." It left her lips as a whispered statement.

It was his turn to be confused. Why wouldn't he mean what he'd said?

"Here." He reached out an arm to her. "Let me escort you in. I am, after all, acting as professional welcomer, pseudo-host, while my brother entertains inside."

She stared at his kind gesture with wide, timid eyes.

He frowned down at her, concerned. Had he pursued her so aggressively that she was now fearful of his touch? Surely not. He snatched her hand from her side and wrapped her arm around his, pulling her close.

Gwen gasped at the quick movement.

"I know you're new to these kind of events, but when a gentleman asks to escort you, this is what he means." Blake smiled. He couldn't help but tease her.

"Are you calling yourself a *gentleman*?" Her voice was breathy as she offered him a small smile.

He used her trapped arm to pull her closer, forcing her side against his. Leaning his face close to hers, he smirked.

"Would you care to question otherwise?"

Only inches away, her green eyes stared into his soul, captivating him. Suddenly, something ignited in them. Her gaze darkened with glowing desire. In a split second, she'd stolen the remaining space between them and pressed her delicious mouth to his.

Blake's eyes rolled closed in pure ecstasy as her passionate kiss enveloped his senses. Her gentle tongue demanded entry and caressed his own with such fervor that he could no longer control the building erection in his pants.

He'd had just about decided to throw her over his shoulder and take her to his room to make nightlong love to her, when she broke the kiss abruptly. She stepped out of his arms.

"I'm sorry." Her voice was meek, almost ashamed.

Blake fought to catch his breath. "Don't be, love," he told her.

"I don't know what's wrong with me, Blake." She shook her head, as if trying to gather her thoughts. "Clearly I don't know what's good for me."

He gazed at her with concern. Why was she punishing herself? It was obvious they wanted the same thing. "What do you mean, love?"

Gwen stared up at him apologetically. "I don't mean to contradict myself. I meant what I said." She frowned. "At least I think I did. I just find you so—"

Blake waited for her to continue, but she sighed in frustration.

"I should go in. I'm sorry."

And with that she left him, heading away from the entry to the din of the Christmas celebration beyond.

Blake released a deep breath, part in exasperation, part in elation. This proved it. Her kiss proved him right. He wasn't pushing her away, scaring her with his desire to win her over. No. It seemed he had already touched her heart as she had touched his. Yet she was still fighting against her feelings. Maybe she was still struggling to trust him, to believe his love was genuine? Or maybe she really believed she owed David some preference to her heart? Either way, he had to prove to her what she had just proved to him: that their love was mutual and fighting the truth of their feelings was futile.

CHAPTER ELEVEN

An hour had passed and Gwen was still mortified by her behavior. How was she supposed to expect Blake to respect her wish for friendship, when she couldn't even control herself around him? She felt like such a hypocrite. It didn't seem to matter that she had their best interests at heart, or at least hers and David's, anyway. She still feared that her contradictions, her lack of control over her desires, would soon cause Blake to see her as a manipulative tease. But what could she do?

She knew exactly what she had to do—what she had been doing for the past hour: she had to stay away from Blake Davenport.

The festivities of the evening were well underway. Drinks were being consumed at an alarming rate, while the fancy buffet of food set up in the adjacent dining room was just barely matching the alcohol intake. Though it was still early in the evening, some guests had already set free of their senses, while others were determined to be free of their clothes. On the balcony, a group of older gentlemen sang Christmas carols dissonantly while their young, buxom female plus-ones had stripped to their underwear, or lack thereof, and jumped in the pool. Faced with the nude view, Gwen was grateful that Emily had been sent away to have Christmas with her mother in Brisbane and that David had clearly made the function an adult affair. Children should never have to witness naked gold-diggers using their implants as floatation devices. Even Gwen wished she could erase the image.

As she took a sip of her red wine, Gwen turned her attention back inside. For a moment, as though fate was mocking her, her gaze met Blake's. She was quick to look away.

"Are you all right, Gwen? You look like you've just seen an ex."

Abigail Rickards—latest weather girl for the ABC—touched Gwen's arm gently.

Gwen offered her a reassuring smile. "Fine, Abby."

Though David was once again lost in the sea of guests, he had made a point of greeting Gwen as she'd entered the room. He'd made a few compliments about her outfit and then quickly introduced her to the short, voluptuous, bleached blonde who now stood beside her. Apparently "Abby", as she wished to be called, didn't know anyone else either and so, was grateful to find a buddy to stick to for the rest of the evening, or at least until she was drunk enough to let Bradley—the sports reporter from Channel Seven—take her home.

Gwen drank the rest of her wine in a final gulp. She was going to need another glass if she hoped to make it through until the end of the evening. Stopping a waitress, she swapped her empty glass for a full one and took another swig.

"Are you sure you didn't see an ex, hun? You're drinking like you just saw an ex."

Gwen shook her head. "No. I'm fine, really. Tell me more about this Bradley guy."

"Oh, okay. Well, like I said, we used to date, you know." Abby continued to prattle on.

Distracted by her own predicament, Gwen took

another sip as her new acquaintance's voice became a garbled mass of sound. She wondered where David was. She knew that as host, he was probably obligated to perform like a social butterfly all evening; she just wished that some of that social interaction might involve her. But it appeared as though she wouldn't be so lucky. How was she supposed to keep her promise to herself about giving him a chance by getting to know him better, when she could barely get a moment alone with him? It seemed like an impossible dilemma that only her wine glass could solve.

"Mr. Davenport stares at you a great deal, Gwen." Abby's curious tone cut through Gwen's thoughts.

"Who? David?" Gwen glanced around hopefully.

Perhaps Abby had spotted him through the horde of sloshed B-grade celebrities, egotistical multi-millionaires, and eccentric billionaires. Gwen would have guessed that he might be on the terrace by the canal with the popular crowd, the A-grade stars, who had disappeared down there earlier. But she hoped she was wrong. She really needed the opportunity to talk to him properly, for them to have the chance to open up to each other.

Abby shook her head and pointed conspicuously through the crowd. "No. The younger one. The photographer."

Gwen was following Abby's gaze before she had a chance to realize her mistake. Her eyes locked with Blake's. From across the room, his dark, lustful stare smoldered through her. It sent a quiver of tingling sensations down her body. She forced herself to look away.

"I can't think why, unless he means to tease me." Gwen shrugged and took a sip of her wine. Another glass was almost empty.

"Though we hardly know each other. Perhaps he's looking at you." She forced a smile in Abby's direction.

Abby's expression lit up like a chocoholic at a

chocolate factory. "You really think so? You think I should go say hi?"

Gwen nodded as she held back a chuckle. "By all means, please, do what you have to do."

Excitedly, Abby hurried away from her, pushing her way petitely through the tall crowd in the direction of Blake's last known coordinates. It seemed a shame to tell her that he was already on the move, ducking out of this room and into another. But Gwen was grateful to have a moment alone. Her holiday celebrations had become much more stressful than expected after finding herself torn between the advances of two brothers: one who would be quick to take advantage if she'd decided against wearing knickers and another who seemed barely interested either way.

Gwen stifled a laugh and drank the last of her wine. She really needed to find another wine-bearing waitress. As she pushed her way past a group of older gentlemen whose high alcohol intake had removed all inhibitions and any knowledge of personal space, she felt a rogue slap to her behind. Hearty laughter ensued. She spun around and shot them with a glare. She was just about to open her mouth to scold them in her best teacher speech, when the deep tones of a familiar voice interrupted her.

"Apologize to the lady." Blake had a firm grip on the wrist of one of the men.

Gwen could only assume it was the one who had slapped her.

All laughter ceased and the men in the circle looked concerned. Blake stood taller than all of them, towering over them with his dark features and threatening stare.

"We were only playing around, mate," one of the men piped up. He looked genuinely apologetic.

"Yeah, sorry, Blakey-boy," said the man whose wrist Blake was crushing. "We got a bit carried away, you know. Didn't realize she was with you."

Blake released him and smiled. "She is, Frank. So, now

you know." He snatched Gwen's hand possessively.

Immediately, she tried to break free of him, but his grasp was firm and unmoving. She continued to struggle against him, but he just ignored her.

"If you boys are still hoping for some easy fun, I'd try the pool." Blake winked at them. It was clear that he thought sending them to a pool full of glamour models was a safe bet for them to get their jollies without getting slapped with a sexual harassment lawsuit.

He nodded a polite farewell and then dragged Gwen away. He stalked through the adjoining dining room, out into the hall, and then tossed Gwen into a vacant study. She stumbled in her high heels, but his grip on her hand steadied her. Blake shut the door behind them. Furious, Gwen tried to tug her hand free. This time, he let her. She stumbled slightly, but recovered and slammed her hands on her hips.

"I am not *with you*," she snapped at him. "You can't just go around telling people that I am."

Blake smirked and crossed his arms over his chest. "You are now. All alone with me."

"Shut up," she told him. It hadn't sounded as forceful as she'd hoped.

Suddenly, she felt a little dizzy. How many glasses of wine had she drunk? She counted three, but red always hit her harder than white. And sculling the last two probably hadn't helped.

Gwen backed up against the huge, intricately carved, mahogany desk behind her and rested her rump on top. Sitting seemed to help and soon the room stopped spinning. When she opened her eyes again, Blake was standing before her, his pants almost touching her silk-covered knees.

"Too much wine, love?" His voice was full of concern.

She nodded ashamedly as he reached forward and brushed a loose curl behind her ear. The rough warmth of his hand cupped her cheek and she rested her head against it. Why was he being so nice to her? She hadn't been very amiable to him. She wished she wasn't so comfortable and content with his tender touch. She gazed up into his eyes.

"What do you want?" Her voice was a relaxed murmur.

"That's not very nice," he teased. "Who just rescued you from a sleazy geezer?"

Gwen smiled playfully. "I could have rescued myself."

"Of course you could, love." Blake's tone humored her.

She lifted her head from his hand. She narrowed her eyes at him as his hand fell away.

"Why did you really bring me in here, Blake?" She couldn't hide the suspicion from her voice.

He frowned. "You're insightful even when you're tipsy. Good to know."

Gwen mirrored his frown. He was clearly keeping something from her.

Sighing, Blake sat on the desk beside her. He grabbed her hand and caressed it comfortingly.

"Remember when I first saw you last night?" He pronounced his words slowly, as though careful not to say the wrong thing.

Gwen nodded. "It feels like weeks ago now."

Blake smiled. "That's because of our chemistry, love."

She glared at him. "I think we've fallen off topic."

His expression became serious and he released another deep sigh. He seemed to be really struggling with what he had to say.

"Yesterday, when you arrived, I went to warn you about my brother."

Gwen's temper flared slightly. For some reason, she felt protective of David, as though she ought to defend him against Blake's accusations. She struggled to leave her hand in his.

She swallowed apprehensively. "Okay."

Blake spun to face her, his dark eyes pleading with her. "Gwen, David is not who you think he is. He does things like this often, things that benefit only him."

"Things like what exactly? Inviting me here for the holidays?" Gwen's voice was sharp. She snatched her hand free of Blake's.

Blake's posture slumped at the obvious rejection. "You don't know him like I do, Gwen. He's looking after his own best interests by inviting you here."

"And you aren't, by telling me this? How do I know you're the one telling the truth?"

Blake shook his head. "You don't, but I'm hoping that you'll be able to make a better informed decision about him after hearing what I have to say."

Gwen thought about his words. She stared at the pain in his expression, the clear internal conflict he was suffering. Every fiber of her being wanted to believe that what he was about to tell her was true. All his emotions seemed so genuine. He couldn't be that clever at lying, could he? Her temper quelled and she realized that, whether he was about to lie or not, she wanted to hear what he had to say.

She slipped her hand back into his. Blake's expression brightened at her gesture.

"Okay, tell me. I'd like to know." She offered him a weak smile in an effort to hide her anxiety.

Blake took a deep breath and began. "What you don't know about my brother is that he is always used to getting his own way. Being born into our wealthy family meant that even as a child, he was spoilt into believing that he could have everything he wanted. From grades at school, to getting into his university preferences and climbing his way up the career ladder...if our late father wasn't pulling strings to get him what he wanted, then David was finding another way to get that to which he felt entitled."

Blake caressed Gwen's hand reassuringly. "What this means, Gwen, is that David almost always has a reason behind why he does something. If he invited you here under the pretense of spending the holidays in a loving family environment instead of the alternative, then you can be sure there is more to his plans than that. You've already discovered that Emily being here was never part of his scheme, though I'm sure he told you otherwise."

He paused as if waiting for Gwen's response.

She nodded. David had implied that his daughter Emily would be spending Christmas and New Year's with them. She couldn't deny the fact that she had been quite surprised upon discovering from Blake that Emily would not be there at all for the celebrations. But she had hoped that there was a simple explanation and that things had just changed unexpectedly. Maybe Emily's mother had wanted to spend the special time of year with her, or vice versa? Or maybe David wanted to make Gwen's time with him a more intimate, romantic occasion? Initially, Gwen had hoped for the latter, but it was evident now that he'd had no such plans.

Blake gazed at her, a look of deep understanding filling his eyes as he watched her.

"As I'm sure you'll soon discover, his plans are more intricate than anything you may have expected." Blake's expression became sympathetic. "Are you aware David and his ex-wife, Michelle, are about to begin a custody battle for Emily?"

"No." Gwen's answer slipped out tentatively.

Blake nodded. "For months now, he's been looking into everything he can do to try to keep the joint custody they agreed upon over a year ago. Even though there is no viable proof to suggest its success, he has decided to arrange a new wife for himself, a new mother for Emily, in the hopes of swaying the court in his favor. In his mind, he believes he may stand a better chance of retaining joint custody if he can show the court that he can offer Emily a stable family life with both a male and female role model to love and care for her."

Blake's expression became even more serious and he narrowed his gaze at her.

"Gwen, that's where you come in. David hopes to marry you to maintain joint custody of Emily."

Gwen's breath caught in her throat. *Marriage? To David?* She claimed she hardly knew Blake, but David was even more of a stranger. Besides the rare greeting-and-farewelling at the school gate when patrolling the carpark on bus duty, she'd only had a very short time to properly chat with him the day before. It was a crazy, inconceivable idea. *Marriage?* She didn't even love him. She didn't even know what her feelings were for him. They were yet to go beyond acquaintances, just slightly more than that of a host and his guest.

Her pulse quickened as her heart raced and she suddenly felt too warm. She pulled her hand gently free from Blake's and wrung her clammy hands together nervously. Eventually, she glanced up at him. Could she really believe all this? It was still Blake's word against David's. Yet in discovering what Blake had to say, David's strange behavior was beginning to make sense.

"What are you thinking, love?" Blake gazed at her with genuine worry.

Gwen's mind was a mess of thoughts. "I don't know."

"I'm sorry, but I had to tell you."

She could hear the anguish in his voice. She nodded. "I understand."

Blake slipped a hand beneath her chin, lifting her face until her green eyes met his.

"I need you to know that I love my brother, even with all his faults. He is *my brother* and I am used to making allowances for him. I usually try to stay out of his business, but in this case, he has gone too far. He could ruin another person's life just to benefit his own. Don't get me wrong, he's a wonderful father. He loves Emily and just wants to do all he can to keep her in his life. But he is going about it all the wrong way."

He frowned as if gathering his thoughts. "Perhaps if he'd decided to tell the woman he intended to marry the truth behind his request before he proposed, maybe then it wouldn't be such a terrible thing. But tricking her into believing that he truly cares for her, letting her believe that their marriage would be real in all meanings of the word, is in no way fair. Are you aware that he still has strong feelings for Michelle?"

Gwen's eyes widened. She shook her head. "No."

"If he could, he would marry her again in a heartbeat." At the thought, a little smile brightened Blake's face.

Though still in shock, now believing her invitation may have been a scam, Gwen couldn't help but be curious. "Then why doesn't he?"

Blake shrugged. "He believes Michelle is the one thing he wants that he cannot have."

Gwen's gaze fell to the floor. It was a sad story, really. No matter how narcissistic and pretentious Blake would have her believe his brother to be, Gwen couldn't help but feel sympathy for David and his predicament. Love was supposed to conquer all.

Standing up from where she had been perched on the desk, Gwen found that the seriousness of their conversation had lessened her tipsiness. The room barely spun at all. She turned to face Blake.

"I think I just need some time," she told him carefully.

His soft smile fell at her words.

Shaking her head, she put a soothing hand on his shoulder. He was quick to grab hold of it with his own hands, as if keeping her in place. He gazed into her eyes.

"I'm not saying I don't believe you," she said. "I just need a moment to process everything. If what you have told me is all true, then I have to re-evaluate some things."

Blake nodded. "Us, maybe?" His voice was hopeful.

She smiled. "I should go. Got to get back to the party…and Abby. She's probably still looking for you."

A curious smirk twisted his lips. "Looking for me?"

Gwen grinned light-heartedly. "Long story."

Drawing her hand from his, Gwen forced a reluctant

Blake to release her once more. Still a little unsteady in her heels and with a final smile, she walked warily to the door. Then she left him, slipping out into the noisy hall still filled with the echoes of loud laughter and music from the adjacent party.

CHAPTER TWELVE

It was nearly ten and the party had only increased in intensity. From its classy beginning, the level of refinement of the function had appeared to deteriorate by the hour. The bar had progressed from wine and champagne to beer and shots of liquor, which appeared to be quite a success with the guests. The once-serene pool was now full of semi- or entirely naked people gyrating against each other to the beat of the music. With the orchestra on break, a trendy local DJ had taken over with a unique sound, a risky mix of Christmas tunes and house music. Though the other guests had taken to the familiar vocals and repetitive beats with overwhelming enthusiasm, Gwen still didn't know what to make of it. The *Little Drummer Boy* now had an awesome drum set.

No wonder the Davenports' Christmas party was such a famous affair. It was only a couple of bouncers and a few dildos away from a sleazy nightclub blended with a drunken orgy. Gwen hoped she could steer clear of both.

Shortly after leaving Blake, Gwen had run into Abby again. Poor Abby had been rather disheartened about missing her chance with the younger Davenport brother, but Gwen had assured her that it was his loss. If he'd just let Gwen be, left her to fend for herself against Frank and his friends, Blake could have easily had a new conquest. Gwen's heart twinged at the thought. It hurt her to think of him with someone else. But she didn't own him, they weren't exclusive, they hadn't even defined what they had. And what was it that they actually had?

Chemistry? Lust? A great desire to see each other naked? Maybe even…love?

Yet how could she be certain of any of it? She had struggled to trust him when all she'd known about him was his reputation in the media, but now upon discovering the lengths his brother would go to in order to get what he wanted, Gwen found herself even more unsure. Was Blake like his brother? What if he only saw her as another conquest? Apparently, David would do anything and everything to achieve his desires. What proof did she have to believe Blake would be any different? Her ex-fiancé had been charming and had said all the right things too, right up until he'd cheated on her. She couldn't risk her heart getting hurt to that same extent again. She'd barely recovered the last time. She didn't know if she could survive another cheater.

"Isn't he yummy?" Abby was staring across the room at Bradley.

She had downed her fourth tequila shot and had taken off her heels, so that she could still stand without swaying. Bradley was eyeing her, too. Obviously, they had both become more appealing with each glass of alcohol consumed.

"If you say so." Gwen couldn't be sure how to answer a question like that, especially one she didn't agree with.

Bradley was of average height, with a crooked jaw and the typical rugby player physique. He had seemed a nice enough person at the beginning of the night, even though he'd become rather boisterous and loud with each swig of beer since then. But he was definitely not Gwen's type. She was grateful he seemed to have eyes only for Abby. The two of them seemed to suit each other. They were sure to make a nicely pickled couple eventually, when one of them had drunk enough Dutch courage to come within speaking distance of the other.

With curiosity distracting Gwen as she tried to remember Abby's comments about their breakup, movement brought her attention to the small platform that had been arranged for the DJ. The raucous crowd parted and David took the stage. Confidently, he motioned to the DJ to cut the music and then addressed the room over a microphone.

"Merry Christmas, everyone! I hope you're all enjoying the party so far."

There was a universal cheer from the room. Even some of the plastic Barbies and their gents in the pool screamed their approval.

Deep inside, Gwen groaned. Was there really still more to come? Perhaps she should start taking advantage of those tequila shots.

"Now, I know you're all dying to get back to the best party of the year."

Bradley and his buddies hooted as though they were cheering from the bleachers at a rugby game.

Acknowledging them with a nod, David continued. "But I've got something very important to do first. There is a wonderful woman in this room tonight who is about to become one very lucky lady."

David searched the crowd, but it only took a moment for his gaze to land on Gwen. He grinned smugly, as though his plans were coming together.

Gwen's stomach dropped. "Oh, shit." She was lucky she'd said it under her breath.

Her heart skipped a beat in terror and her skin grew cold. Like a hare in headlights, with wide eyes, she glanced quickly around the room.

Where is Blake?

"Gwen—"

David's voice had her staring back at him. The crowd dispersed around her, creating a wide, circular cage. Only Abby stayed by her side, buzzing with excitement.

"Beautiful, kind, caring Gwen." David gestured a hand out to her across the swaying heads of intoxicated guests. "I know we've only known each other for a short time, but in seeing my daughter's affection for you, I, myself, have begun to share her love for you. In winning my daughter's heart, you have also won my own."

His hand slipped into his tuxedo jacket and there was a collective gasp from the crowd. Even some of the naked pool bunnies had slinked up to the balcony to catch a glimpse of the drama unfolding.

Gwen was sure she couldn't have looked more terrified, though she fought to put on a brave face.

With gift in hand, David stepped from the stage and strode toward her. As though parting the inebriated sea, people trickled out of David's way, giving him room to find and enter Gwen's inner circle. When he dropped to his knee, the horde of guests continued to offer appropriate sound effects.

But their hum of awe was wasted on Gwen. Her brain had abandoned her and she had lost all feeling in her limbs. Had her muscles and joints not been locked in absolute fright, she probably would have tumbled to the floor.

David took her malleable hand in his. "Gwen, I know I don't have much to offer you."

His false modesty brought laughter from the onlookers.

"Only a luxury mansion by the Noosa canals, a holiday villa in the South of France, anything you wish for that money can buy, but most importantly, the love and devotion of a daughter and her doting father."

The multitude of guests hung on his every word, laughing when he expected, sighing when he wanted, and even awwing when he needed. It seemed almost scripted. Clearly, David was enjoying being the crowd's center of attention a little too much.

While Gwen was petrified at what was yet to come—knowing full well that she was about to refuse her host's proposal in front of all his gossiping guests—David's behavior just confirmed everything Blake had told her earlier. Yet she still couldn't decide if Blake's honesty about his brother actually proved the sincerity of his feelings for her, or if it only meant he shared his brother's talent for deceit.

"Gwen—"

A gold ring with a huge diamond appeared in David's hand.

"Will you do me the honor of becoming my wife?"

Gwen tried desperately to think of a nice way of rejecting David in front of their large, unpredictable audience. Yet the pressure of the situation had her hearing the crickets of emptiness, proving that all intelligence had left her. She glanced around the grinning glut of guests.

Where is Blake?

"Yes!"

The word had come from so close to her that she almost believed her own voice had betrayed her.

"Yes, she will!"

It was Abby. Her four tequila shots had taken over and she was now running the show. She snatched the ring from David's hand and thrust it on Gwen's finger.

"Whoo!" Her cheer encouraged the others and the proposal was complete.

Gwen was still in shock when David embraced her. His lips barely brushed hers before he cradled her in a hug. She couldn't move. What had just happened?

It was from within David's arms that Gwen finally spied Blake. He was across the room, only meters away. He was seething, almost vibrating with anger. His eyes shot daggers into his brother's back. When his livid gaze met Gwen's, it altered slightly, becoming a fiery combination of rage, jealousy, and lust.

Gwen felt a sudden pang of fear. She hoped Blake had been witness to what had actually happened. She prayed he knew that she didn't purposely choose his devious brother over him. It hurt her heart to think of him believing she'd so openly rejected him.

With a brief kiss to the cheek and a whispered promise to find her later, David removed himself from her person and went to celebrate with the exhilarated partygoers.

Gwen was frozen. Her gaze locked onto Blake's, unmoving. She was aware of the circle around her closing in, as all manner of female guests came to gaze in awe at the ring on her hand. She was even sure she felt the tickle of many manicured fingers, like a hundred tarantula legs, join together to lift her hand from her side. But she couldn't look at them. Her eyes remained focused on Blake.

His dark, ferocious stare grew larger and larger until—

"Excuse me, ladies." Blake's deep voice sliced through the high-pitched chirping of the women around her.

Without hesitation, his strong hand grasped Gwen's upper arm tightly and he began dragging her through the tight circle of envious, awestruck women. Catty comments erupted in their wake.

"Isn't that the brother?"

"What? She gets them both?"

"Who is this *Gwen* person, anyway?"

"Hi, Blake!"

But neither Gwen nor Blake turned to acknowledge them. Gwen had only one thing on her mind: convincing Blake that she hadn't said yes to David, and Blake, too, seemed to share a singular focus. Gwen only wished she knew what it was.

CHAPTER THIRTEEN

Blake opened the door to Gwen's guest room and pushed her inside. He shut and locked it behind them. Gwen stumbled awkwardly in her heels, but made it to the bed before she took a tumble. Flustered, she spun around and sat on the edge of the mattress.

His domineering demeanor was beginning to aggravate her. So what if she was now engaged to Blake's Machiavellian brother, by no fault or agreement of her own? So what if he wasn't happy about it? Neither was she. She glared up at him. She wished he would just say something.

Blake took off his tuxedo jacket and tossed it to the floor. His fingers ripped at his black tie, pulling it free of his collar. He threw it across the room.

Gwen's eyes widened. What did he think he was doing?

Undoing the first few buttons of his white shirt, he strode toward her.

Gwen's breath became harsh and her pulse quickened. She was caught between a confusion of emotions: fear, anger...desire. Her body began to tingle all over at the thought of what might happen when he reached her. She bit her lip, fighting the urge to yell at him to go away and her longing to beg for him to come closer. She was sure that initiating either conversation wouldn't end well for her.

Blake's stare remained stern as he reached the bed. He towered above her for a moment, his presence almost foreboding, before dropping to his knees before her.

Gwen flinched at his action. She didn't know what to expect next.

Kneeling in front of her, Blake brushed his fingers over her silk-covered knees. Delicately, his hands began to creep up along her thighs. The ticklish feeling sent warm, tingling sensations higher, to a place Gwen craved for him to touch. She bit down hard, savaging her lower lip to stave off a moan. Blake's gaze had seemed focused on his movement until that moment. But now his dark stare held hers.

His hands rose free of her, then snatched up her left hand. Again, she flinched at his swift motion. Half of her wished to flee, as if seeing danger in his eyes, while the rest desperately anticipated what might yet be to come.

Gwen watched Blake carefully as he glared at the glittering atrocity on her ring finger. His gaze quickly returned to hers. With a sly smirk, he quirked an eyebrow as if in challenge. He stared at her as he separated her elegant fingers to better reveal the tainted extremity. Then his mouth covered her skin, capturing her finger into a sweet, soft abyss. Gwen's breath caught in her throat. The feeling of his hot, wet mouth on her skin had her imagining it licking and sucking its way across more sensitive parts. Her insides quivered at the thought and she felt moisture pool between her legs. She fought back another feminine gasp.

Blake's tongue caressed her finger seductively as though suggesting the use of his skills elsewhere. His smug gaze bore into her as she struggled not to writhe her hips against the firm mattress beneath her. She couldn't believe how turned on she was. Had he kissed those luscious lips to her most intimate region at that moment, she was sure she would explode.

All of a sudden, his lips sank to her knuckle and a sharp, involuntary cry escaped Gwen's throat. Pointedly, Blake's teeth locked gently behind David's engagement ring. Then slowly, tantalizingly, he used his supple mouth and the light nip of teeth to slide the ring free of her finger. As his lips left her skin, her whole body yearned for more. She was all but ready to pounce on his lap, tear off his clothes, and devour him with kisses. Yet she restrained her desire, holding her safe, virtuous position on the bed. In vain, she tried to calm her ragged breathing and steady the blood rushing excitedly through her veins.

Gwen had to get a hold of herself. Though she was entirely besotted with Blake and a natural passion seemed to blaze between them like a second sun, she still couldn't be certain of his true desires. Were his actions due to a possessive jealously brought on by the strong feelings he'd confessed for her? Was his affection for her as real and true as her own for him? Or was this whole act of seduction brought on by a darker desire, by a need to ruin his brother's plans, seize that which David wanted, and claim another innocent conquest? All of her instincts doubted the latter. But they had been wrong before. Her barely mended broken heart was testament to that.

Blake's dark brown eyes held her gaze, completely unaware of Gwen's inner turmoil. Through gritted teeth, he bared the diamond ring of false promises, showing it off to her like a prize. Gwen gazed as his moist mouth, his teeth holding the sparkling trinket so delicately, and soon found her imagination forming lustful thoughts against her will. Though only physically and metaphorically free of the jeweled symbol that could define her future forever, Gwen finally felt as though she was permitted to dismiss David and all he offered her. Gazing at Blake, she now knew what she wanted. She was at liberty to discover his true feelings in an effort to explore her own.

Blake stared at her. As if getting the reaction he'd hoped for, his lips curled skyward in a satisfied grin. Then tilting his head away, he spat the sullied object across the room. It tinkled against the tiles as it landed somewhere in the en-suite. Gwen followed its trajectory and then glanced back at Blake. His seductive stare captivated her once more.

"You said yes." It was a loaded statement in an almost threatening tone.

Gwen's eyes widened. "No. No, I didn't." Her innocent voice turned high-pitched in defense.

"That's not what everyone downstairs believes." Blake's dark eyes narrowed on her.

"Maybe not, but it's the truth. *I* never agreed to the proposal." Gwen's face flushed as she became flustered.

Fear gripped her heart at the thought of him believing otherwise. She couldn't bear to have wounded him over such an inaccuracy, have him injured at the idea of her rejecting his advances for David. Even if he was the womanizing playboy the media had labeled him, she still couldn't handle the thought of hurting him or his feelings in such a profound way. He meant too much to her, even in the friendship that had blossomed between them, for her to want to cause him that much pain.

Blake raised an eyebrow at her. "Then you won't marry David." It was a firm statement, intimidating, almost a command.

Gwen shook her head quickly. "No."

He grinned. "Because of me." Again, it was a hard statement.

His words took her by surprise. Though Blake had played a pivotal role in informing her of David's scheme and had therefore helped direct her to her decision, he was not solely responsible for her intended refusal. Of course, Gwen's mind and body were already infatuated with longing for Blake, but without knowing his true character, that was not enough to have forced her decision, either.

She wasn't about to add flame to the fire of his ego, by agreeing that he, in all his perfection, had compelled her to choose to reject his brother. Especially when it wasn't the *entire* truth.

In seeing the smugness on his face, as though he was confident he didn't even need a verbal answer to prove him correct, Gwen became irritated. Blake's arrogance made her want to avoid giving him any pleasure in the idea that he had played any large part in her choice. His haughty expression only seemed to encourage her belief that this was just a big game to him, spoiling his brother's scheme by seducing the woman David had hoped to trick into marriage. The thought made her furious. Had this just been one big competition? Was she just a prize to them both?

She glared at him. "Just because you drag me around this place as though you own me, doesn't mean you do or that I would do anything just because you tell me to."

Before her words had time to sink in, she pushed herself free from the bed and shot past him. She had hoped to make it to the door, but was interrupted in her second step.

Blake was on his feet, his hand gripping her arm tightly, before spinning her around. The force propelled her into his arms, her hands pressed against the hard muscle of his chest. Her face was close to his, foreheads almost touching. They both stared toward the ground as though one glance at each other, in that instant, would ignite something unstoppable.

Gwen could barely catch her breath. She was frightened and furious, but the spicy fragrance of his cologne mixed with his natural musky scent was tremendously enticing, and her body reacted accordingly. His hands held her upper arms in a vice-like grip, holding her in place against him. She bit her lip as their eyes met, their noses touching in a brief, sensual Eskimo kiss. Her whole body thrummed with anticipation, her hands desperate to wander and her hips longing to grind a little closer. Blake made his lips brush against hers and she felt her body quiver at the sensitive touch.

"Why do you always run from me?" His voice was strained.

Gwen moved her head slightly, their noses brushing once more. She closed her eyes for a second to revel in the multitude of sensations. "Because you irritate me so."

He smiled. "Love, you're only irritated because you care."

"No," she lied.

How dare he sound so cocky! How could he possibly claim to understand my feelings?

With a weak effort, she tried to push free of him. "I'm irritated because I don't know what you really want from me."

His expression fell serious. "I want you Gwen. Just you." His voice was soft in its innocent sincerity.

Had she heard that right? Had he just proved her point? That he only wanted her as another notch on his bedpost? Gwen frowned angrily, ignoring the tiny voice of sense that suggested his love might be true. She'd just heard the truth, he wanted her because he couldn't have her, and that was that. Wasn't it?

She slapped her hands against his chest furiously and struggled against him. "Let me go!"

He held her tighter. "That's not going to happen."

When he still wouldn't release her, she slumped against him in exhaustion, her hands spread against his chest and her face cradled beside his neck. He released his grip on her arms and hugged her affectionately.

"I don't want you to hurt me." Her timid voice was weary.

Suddenly, he released her from the embrace. He stepped back to look at her face.

"Did I hurt you?" His concerned expression was full of dread.

Gwen shook her head. "No, but you probably will."

As though taken aback by her words, Blake laughed. It was an awkward sound of disbelief.

"You can't really mean that?" His deep voice posed the question incredulously.

Annoyed by his inappropriate response and free of his grasp, Gwen dashed away from him, this time in the opposite direction. She almost made it to the French doors of the room's private balcony.

Blake caught her hand at the last moment and pulled her to him as he stepped toward her. He gripped her securely in another tender embrace.

"Stop running away from me," he told her. This time it was a firm order.

She shot him a defiant stare. "Don't laugh at me, then."

He shook his head as though he couldn't quite understand why she was so upset with him and he drew her closer. Slipping his arms behind her back, he held her body against his.

Blake smiled compassionately. "Love, you need to start making sense."

She scowled at him. "You say you care, but how can I believe you? You could be just like David. How can I trust that you're any different? That you don't just see me as an object, something to own or conquer?"

Gwen breathed out a frustrated sigh as she finished. She felt utterly drained by the passionate feelings that stirred within her. One moment she hated Blake, the next it could've been love and then again, there was further frustration.

At Gwen's flurry of feelings, Blake's expression became serious, as though he'd suddenly realized the true topic of conversation. His fingers at her back tenderly caressed her soft, bare skin.

"Gwen, I could spend hours telling you that you should believe me, that you should trust me, that I'm nothing like my brother and that I honestly, deeply care for you. I could tell you how wonderful you are, how much my life has changed in knowing you and how much you now mean to me. I could say that I want you, that I've never wanted anyone more, that I need you in my life, and even that I love you."

He gazed lovingly into her green eyes. "But nothing I *say* is enough to convince you of the truth in my words. I don't think you'll believe me until you are ready to. All I can promise you is that I will do everything I can to show you, to help prove to you that I am worthy of your trust and your love."

Gwen's gaze had narrowed on Blake's as she tried to really listen to what he had to say. Though she heard every extraordinary word and though she desperately wanted to believe he meant everything he'd said, a tiny part of her—the part that feared her heart would once again be broken—was terrified that it was all too good to be true. With David no longer in the picture as a viable excuse for her to keep her distance from Blake, she was both left free to pursue and risk a possible relationship with him if she chose to. The concept was both terribly exciting and petrifyingly scary.

In the warmth of his caring, passionate embrace, it took her merely a moment to make a decision.

"Show me how?"

Gwen had only seconds to notice that Blake's smile in reply held a suggestive promise before his lips fell to hers. His kiss was gentle as it smothered her mouth amorously. His tongue, like soft velvet, explored and caressed her. Gwen relaxed into his embrace, giving herself over to her desire. Her hands slipped up his chest and around his neck. She ran her fingers through his short, dark mane as she began to kiss him back with fervor. His hands at the bare skin of her back skimmed a warm, ticklish line around the border of her dress. Suddenly, they slipped beneath the emerald silk and grasped the curve of her rump, pressing her groin firmly against his hard erection.

As a moan escaped her lips, Blake's kiss deepened and Gwen found she couldn't contain herself anymore. Sliding her hands between them, she clawed at his buttons before pulling his shirt out of his pants and ripping it from his shoulders. As if reluctantly, Blake's hands crept free of her dress and he quickly rid himself of his shirt. Gwen had already started on his belt buckle when she felt him momentarily grin into her kiss, as though pleased with her eagerness to undress him.

Blake's sneaky fingers returned to Gwen's back and crisscrossed over her bare skin, working their way higher and higher, until they eventually reached the spaghetti straps of her dress. There they waited as if uncertain, as if expecting to be prevented from their immoral mission. When Gwen paused to gaze up at him, hesitating only to aid his goal, Blake delicately slipped the straps over her shoulders. The silk dress slid down the curves of her body to the floor. He gazed over her, all bare breasts, lace panties, and high heels, and a wicked hunger flared in his dark eyes.

Blake took Gwen into his arms again and pressed her close. His hands roamed over her delicious curves as his mouth covered hers. When his body forced her back a step, she obeyed. He kissed and nipped a hot trail across her jaw and down her neck. Gwen struggled to catch her breath. She moaned at the sensation of his talented lips devouring her. His hot breath on her damp skin sent goosebumps racing down her body, turning her nipples hard and igniting a pleasurable twinge between her thighs. He pushed her back another step, then another. Her body did as he instructed.

Gwen's hands slipped between them, hoping to strip him of his pants. But again her body was ordered to step backward. As she did so, the bare skin of her back met the cool wood and glass of the balcony's French doors. She gasped at the new sensation, the coolness so unexpected against the heat of her skin. Blake's body cornered her there, his hips grinding against her as his lips savaged her mouth.

The firmness of the door gave way suddenly as Gwen realized Blake's fingers were on the door handle. She stumbled out onto the dark balcony and he followed, capturing her mouth in another kiss before she could escape.

Outside, the noisy ruckus continued, with the pool below now full of intoxicated guests. The horrible mix of techno and caroling raged on against the cacophony of laughter and wannabe karaoke stars.

Gwen broke free of the kiss in an effort to glance behind her, fearing that anyone below might be able to see. But Blake wouldn't let her get away.

On the large, darkened balcony, he pushed her back gently against a decorative Grecian column, hiding her from the sight of the revelers below. As she opened her mouth to question him, he stifled her silent words with a kiss. Her arms wrapped around him, pulling his body hard against hers. Gwen melted into the embrace as Blake's tongue stroked hers attentively. She was so easily distracted by her body's desperate craving for him to kiss her, to touch her, to be inside her.

With nipples hard, her plump breasts grazed against the bare muscles of his chest, sending tingles of sensation to her sensitive nether region. Blake's hips rocked against hers, pressing the length of his erection against her and forcing a high-pitched moan from her throat. Pausing just long enough to grin down at her, Blake covered her mouth with a finger, in a shushing manner. With a look of challenge, Gwen spread her lips and slid her mouth over his finger, drawing it deep inside the soft, wet sanctuary. Surprised by her sexy retaliation, Blake's mouth fell open as if the sensation had also struck him elsewhere.

It had been Blake's idea to come outside, after all. If he wanted to play, to tease moans from her lips only to encourage her silence, then Gwen wouldn't hesitate to make his situation equally difficult.

He quirked an eyebrow and then slid his finger free. Tracing a wet line over her chin, down her neck, and between her breasts, his cheeky finger didn't stop until his hand had sneaked beneath the lace of her panties. Her mouth widened in a silent cry, but she refused to make a sound. His playful fingers fondled her there, caressing her, stroking her. Her thighs parted instinctually, giving Blake better access. Then, through the moist softness of her skin, he slipped that cheeky finger inside of her. She yelped in pleasure, then froze, eyes wide at the sound. Blake grinned at her triumphantly.

Together, they listened for a brief moment, as if expecting the world below to have heard the noise and discovered their transgression. Yet still, the partygoers appeared oblivious to their behavior.

Blake's grin widened and his finger moved gently inside of her. Gwen gasped at the sensation and bit her lip to prevent another cry. Overwhelmed by the thrilling feeling of his long finger caressing the softness deep inside her, she closed her eyes for a second. Clinging desperately to his bare back with claw-like hands, she forced him as close as was humanly possible. As she did so, his finger stabbed even deeper inside. Her eyes rolled and her head fell back. Bursts of pleasurable sensation, like tingling fireworks, spread throughout her body.

Gwen moved to kiss him, desperate to feel his gentle mouth devouring hers, but Blake had other plans. His teeth nipped at her neck as his finger dove slowly in and out, in and out then back inside her. Her pleasure was building unbearably, his rhythm purposely slow and steady, as if to build and control her release at his will. His mouth continued its attention down along her soft skin, pausing at a swollen breast and taut nipple to lick and nibble her sensitive flesh. He dropped to his knees before her, maintaining his rhythmic motion inside her as he placed gentle kisses over and then beyond her navel. As he reached the lace of her panties, he withdrew his finger from her aching insides, forcing her to stave off a desperate moan, and then slid his hand from her underwear. Blake's hands gripped Gwen's hips as his tongue flicked out across the lacy rim, slipping teasingly below the fabric. She sighed, her eyes closing as her hands crept up from his shoulders to clench in the thick, dark fullness of his hair.

Blake's fingers caught the lace of her panties and pulled them down the length of her slender legs. She stepped out of them, kicking them to the side. Gwen gazed down the line of her naked body at him, staring into the hunger blazing in the depths of his dark brown eyes. She had a moment to realize that she didn't feel vulnerable or scrutinized by his lustful stare, but invigorated, powerful, and exceptionally sexy, before his skillful mouth kissed her skin again.

While his hands caressed the curves of her buttocks, Blake's lips covered her swollen clit. Gwen gasped at the powerful sensation. His tongue swirled around, licking her delicate nub as his lips suckled at the sensitive flesh. Her fingers clenched in his hair as she tried to control herself and the desirous sounds of pleasure that wanted to escape her throat.

As his kiss slid lower, his tongue stroking over layers of soft skin, he grabbed her right leg demandingly and draped it over his shoulder. Gwen shuddered. Her eyes closed and her head fell back as Blake's tongue searched deeper. His mouth explored her velvety flesh until his tongue struck her core. She yelped in pleasure, unable to contain the sound inside. Like a repetitive dance, his tongue slid deeper inside her, then licked swirling circles around her supple entry before his mouth devoured her, sucking against the center of all pleasure. As his mouth repeated his hungry pursuit, quickening the rhythm, the overwhelming sensations began to build and build and build. Gwen reached a place where the pleasure felt so good it was almost painful. She cried out in an irresistibly devastating release as it burst like a million sensitive little explosions, tingling through her, cascading throughout her body in waves. Her whole body shuddered with the last few quivers of sensation.

After one last, affectionate kiss, Blake's mouth withdrew from her swollen flesh. Gwen gazed down at him lovingly as he gently released her leg from his shoulder. She was still thrumming with passion, aching with hypersensitivity, tingling at every breath, but completely, utterly warm with contentment. Blake's gratified smile was a match for her stupidly happy grin. No man before him had ever made her feel so completely uninhibited, so overwhelmed with pleasure. She was just about to slump to her knees beside him, eager to repay his exceptional effort with a few tricks of her own, when there was a knocking sound from inside the room.

"Gwen."

Silence.

The knocking began again. "Gwen. Are you in there?"

It was David.

.

CHAPTER FOURTEEN

Blake hadn't wanted to release his grip on Gwen's arm. His fear that they would never again be as close as they had been in that moment was unfounded. Yet his disappointment that their interlude would be at an end as soon as that door opened was factual and heart-wrenching. Blake wasn't ready to leave her tonight. He didn't want their time together to come to an end and he was certain she felt the same.

He had purposely stopped her from immediately reacting to David's call, hoping to keep her from making the obvious mistake of granting David attention he didn't deserve. Blake had even considered holding her down and ravishing her, seducing her luscious body, his lips finding her sweet spot once more, in the hope of convincing her to stay in his arms. But her beautiful, green eyes had pleaded with him and he was powerless against that look to hold her against her will. For some reason, she wanted to answer, wanted to acknowledge David's interruption and for some reason, Blake eventually let her.

He had hoped she'd been as enraptured in the moment as he was, but her good manners and kind heart seemed to win out. Had she agreed, Blake would have easily had them ignore his brother's existence for the rest of the evening, lavishing each other in carnal pleasures until daybreak. He hated the idea of allowing David to have any power over their relationship, disrupting their sensual discovery of each other with a simple knock. Blake regretted not holding her closer. He regretted letting her leave to face David alone. But he could not have refused her stunning eyes when they'd implored him to release her. He had felt too captivated, too compelled, not to obey.

Before the interruption, Blake had been exhilarated, feeling as though he'd finally been making headway with Gwen. He was certain he was starting to get through to her—at least on some level—that he truly cared for her as she did for him. And Gwen had finally started to relax, as though liberated in his loving embrace. She'd even begun to accept her desires, her feelings, and possibly even his feelings for her. She had actually started opening up to him physically, even emotionally, trusting him—at the very least with her delectable body. It had been so overwhelming for him to finally begin to show her how he felt. Their sensational chemistry had been so deliciously satisfying that when the moment ended, Blake had been struck with such an irrational feeling of foreboding terror. It was as if he feared that interrupting this thrilling mixture of love, passion, and contentment might then mean losing it forever. He knew the mere thought was illogical, but it didn't suppress his dread.

Buckling his belt as he stood, Blake cursed his brother's self-serving impulses and terrible timing. Why was he not still occupied with his drunk, boorish guests downstairs? From all the din and commotion by the pool below, the party appeared to be as wild as earlier and, as host, it was David's job to remain in the fray, if only in an effort to control it. The furor of laughter and shouting proved he had not been entirely successful in that role. Blake had to wonder, what had sent David searching for Gwen in the first place? What had led him to look upstairs? Had he seen Blake with her?

Stepping closer to the French doors leading inside the room, Blake ensured that he remained hidden in the darkness of the balcony. He had obeyed Gwen's instructions, waiting unseen outside for her while she bravely answered the door. Yet his patience was waning and his trepidation at the thought of her facing David alone was growing.

She had disappeared only minutes before, but it felt like an hour. Peering secretly through the glass panes, Blake could see her standing by the bedroom door. Somehow she had managed to slip into her dress just quick enough to answer before the knocking ceased. As though purposely hiding Blake's strewn shirt and jacket on the bedroom floor, Gwen held the door only slightly ajar. Listening carefully, Blake could hear her sweet, but breathy voice greet his brother.

As he watched them, their voices hardly distinguishable against the ruckus of the Christmas celebration downstairs, he saw David push his way into the room. Gwen staggered backward, letting the door fly free of her hands before it hit the wall. His brother stared at Gwen, his expression appeared stern, but concerned—perhaps worried his scheme wasn't going accordingly. When he moved toward her, she backed away cautiously. David's expression morphed from puzzled to suspicious when he glanced around the room and his passing gaze took obvious note of the shirt and jacket on the floor. Blake watched his brother's posture straighten and become more formal. It was obvious that he now meant serious business. Fearing for Gwen under his brother's harsh scrutiny, Blake could no longer stay hidden. Whether she wanted him to help or not, he wouldn't stand by and watch David tear strips off Gwen for something his brother had no honest, moral right to be furious about.

Striding into the room from the balcony, shirtless in only tuxedo pants and dress shoes, Blake didn't stop until he was beside Gwen.

David's nostrils flared furiously as he scowled at Blake. "Nice of you to take your time to join us, brother." David's sarcasm didn't hide his anger.

"Couldn't find my shirt." Blake glared at his brother and returned his sarcastic tone.

Gwen's gorgeous eyes were large, as though fearful there would be conflict. She glanced worriedly between the two of them. When her gaze returned to his, Blake gave her a soft, reassuring smile and took her hand.

David snorted haughtily as the sight of them. "You're so predictable, Blake."

Blake glowered at his brother. "How so?" His voice was almost a growl.

Crossing his arms, David glared down his nose at them. "No sooner are you told not to do something than you do it. Perhaps I should have said, 'tell her everything, Blake' and then you would have done the opposite."

Clenching his jaw in resentment, Blake felt his upper lip quiver toward a snarl. If his brother wanted a fight, he could easily give him one.

David waved a hand in their general direction. "So, I have to deal with this now, do I." He hadn't posed it as a question and apparently, he had no intention of waiting for an answer from either of them. His stare burned lividly into Blake's. "I'm always cleaning up your indiscretions."

Blake took an aggressive step forward. "I think you'll find this is your indiscretion, brother, not mine. I told you how I felt about Gwen. I warned you not to cross me, and all before your grand proposal. You did this to yourself."

David gestured to the strewn clothing on the ground and then bared his teeth angrily at Blake. "Oh, clearly!" It was said with such bitter sarcasm. "No, Blake, I think you'll find my only mistake was in trusting you. I should never have asked you to stay for the holidays. Some brother you are."

Blake took another hostile step forward, his hands

clenching to fists in a threatening manner as he broke free of Gwen. But before he could explode and growl expletives at David, Gwen had grabbed Blake's arm again and stepped in front of him.

"I'm very grateful you invited him." Gwen's voice was bold and unwavering as she took a stand against David.

"Of course you are, missy." His gaze shot to Blake's naked chest insinuatingly and then back to her. "I had expected more of you, as well. I had been so sure a poor, primary school teacher would have chosen money over sex."

Gwen's jaw dropped at the insult. "Excuse me!"

Blake inched forward, but Gwen's firm hold on his arm kept him from laying the punch his brother deserved.

"Don't play coy," David growled at her. "You two clearly deserve each other. You both share the troublesome talent of making decisions based on emotion."

"That's because we're both human and we both have a heart!" Gwen's voice was deepened with anger. "I'm very grateful you invited Blake, David," she hissed at him again. "Had he not been here to warn me and protect me from your plans, I would be engaged to you right now with only the future of a loveless marriage before me."

He scoffed at her. "I think you're forgetting something, missy. You *are* engaged to me."

Releasing her grip on Blake, Gwen held her naked left hand out to him.

David's eyes widened. "Where's the ring!" His voice was like a roar.

"Guess that means the engagement's off." Blake spat smugly.

David was utterly enraged. His eyes glared at them ferociously. His lips quivered into a snarl. Then, all of a sudden, with a calming breath, his posture relaxed.

As he grinned at them with disdain, fear gripped Blake's heart and he mentally cursed himself for not comprehending the true extent of his brother's scheme. As an exceptional businessman, David always had every angle covered. Blake could see the proof of it in his brother's haughty expression. It hadn't mattered whether Blake had intervened or not, whether he'd told Gwen the truth—David already had another strategy to convince Gwen, one way or another, to obey his wishes to get married. Blake could only imagine the kind of blackmail his brother would stoop to in order for Gwen to do as he pleased.

Looking at him, David seemed to recognize his understanding. "You're finally getting it, little brother."

Blake glared at him and grabbed Gwen's hand protectively. "I should have known you'd play dirty, David. You have a choice in all this, you know? You don't have to do this to her."

"Do what?" Gwen's voice slipped out timidly as she glanced worriedly between the brothers.

"Gwen." David said her name lyrically as he took a bold step toward her.

Blake pulled Gwen behind him, placing himself between her and his brother once again.

David just chuckled confidently. "Gwen, you like teaching, don't you?"

Gwen frowned at David, her eyes narrowing, but she didn't answer.

"You enjoy teaching the little children like my Emily, isn't that right?" His tone was painfully condescending in its false sweetness.

She nodded, clearly concerned by the unusual line of questioning.

"And you're fond of Emily in particular, aren't you? Though I'm sure you have a delightful, devoted relationship with all your tiny pupils, don't you?"

Gwen's green eyes glowered at him. "I am very fond of all my students as they are fond of me. What are you getting at, David?"

His huge grin in return resembled that of the Cheshire

Cat. "Only that you are evidently a beloved teacher whose affection for her pupils and her work is one of her greatest assets."

Blake glanced at Gwen's alarmed expression. It was obvious she hadn't expected David to threaten one of the few things she loved so whole-heartedly: her ability to teach.

Seeing her comprehension, David became serious and businesslike. "You enjoy being a primary school teacher. You love doing all that it involves. You want to continue to work in that role. Do as I say, then, and everything will remain as it ever was. Cross me, and with one phone call, I will ensure that you'll never work as a teacher again, in any capacity."

Gwen gasped and gripped Blake's arm tightly, her fingers digging in deeply as though reflecting the pain she was suffering.

He held her closer and scowled at David. "You have no right to do this to her. I won't let you ruin her life to solve your own family issues."

David nodded. "Of course you will, brother. You share any information about our little arrangement, hint anything at anyone other than those involved and then *you'll* be responsible for ending her career. You couldn't do that to her, could you?"

He didn't wait for an answer. It was clear from his expression that David knew he'd won. He brushed his hands together and then offered them a genuine smile.

"Now that we've got that sorted, I expect you both to act accordingly and jump when I say so. I don't want anyone else to find out about your little tryst together."

He feigned a pout as he looked over their furious but solemn faces. "Please cheer up and remember why we're really doing this." David's gaze focused solely on Gwen. "To ensure a loving daddy gets to continue to see his little daughter."

With that, David headed for the door, but not before

one final glance.

"Oh, and Gwen," he said with a shark-like grin. "Find that ring."

CHAPTER FIFTEEN

The warm glow of early morning began to shine through the bedroom windows. Somehow Gwen had made it through the night without shedding a tear. It had helped that Blake had stayed with her. She had been concerned that David might have noticed their continued absence and visited them again, but that had never happened. Perhaps he thought he'd sufficiently terrified them with his threats, at least for one evening. And he wouldn't have been wrong.

David's words had kept her awake most of the night, as she lay on the bed, fully dressed and cradled in Blake's arms.

"Gwen, you like teaching, don't you?"

"Cross me and, with one phone call, I will ensure that you'll never work as a teacher again, in any capacity."

The mere thought of never being able to teach, never being able to watch her students learn and grow, horrified her. She had felt sick in the stomach ever since David had outlined his plan for blackmail. Blake had been right with what he'd told her on her very first night there: Gwen would have done herself an immense favor had she just turned tail and left. Why hadn't she listened to him?

She hugged Blake's arms tighter around her and felt him nuzzle closer to her in his sleep. At the warm, affectionate embrace, she realized what she would have lost if she had left that first night. She would have never been able to get to know Blake.

That thought seemed to frighten her much more than that of losing her beloved career. In the short space of time they had known each other, Blake had become so important to her. Gwen's heart, her body, and most of her mind seemed to share the belief that meeting him might possibly have been the best thing that had ever happened to her. Only that tiny part of her brain that hoped to ensure self-preservation was still concerned about his true intentions. Yet she wondered how she could even entertain any negative thoughts about his personality and his desires. He had stood by her last night, defending her against David with such passion, strength of character, and moral enthusiasm. Then, once his brother had abandoned them to their distress, Blake had made every effort to console her. He had been so compassionate, holding her close and listening to her while she tried to process what had just happened.

Throughout it all, Blake had controlled his ferocious rage at his brother's actions and had shared with her such determination to solve all their problems. He had been so adamant that he would save her from sacrificing herself. Gwen had appreciated everything Blake had said to her, even though she knew she didn't have much hope. Of every kind gesture he had made, Gwen had been most grateful for his soothing embrace. He'd held her in his arms without expectation, without suggestion, with no promise of anything further than cuddling her close while she dealt with the ordeal she faced. It had been almost enough to prove that his feelings for her were genuine and more than enough to show her that she was falling in love with him.

Gwen stepped free of the shower and dried herself with one of the navy bath sheets. It was just after ten and though Blake had left her over an hour ago, she continued to find reasons to hide inside her room. Showering had been last on her list of ideas and she knew that soon she would have to face reality and head downstairs.

Although they had dozed together for a little while longer, upon waking, Blake had agreed with her that it was time for them to separate. Breaking their embrace had been one of the most difficult experiences Gwen had suffered through. She had to physically force her body to leave the sanctuary of his affectionate hug. It seemed certain that, if David had his way, she and Blake might never have another opportunity to share something so genuine and truly loving again. The thought was heartbreaking, but so too was the thought of never being able to teach her beautiful, little students again. Neither loss was an option to her. She didn't know how she could function, how she could exist in life without experiencing the enjoyment of her occupation and without being able to express the love she had for Blake. Yet she didn't wish to give in to David. She couldn't even fathom the idea of actually marrying him. Surely they could reason some sense into him, make David see that his scheme would not be successful and that there were alternative ways to keep joint custody of Emily. Even as the thought crossed her mind, Gwen knew it was unlikely. If he was prepared to reach the extent of blackmail to ensure his daughter would remain with him, then he was most certainly willing to execute his threats.

"There has to be another way," Gwen mumbled to herself as she wrapped the towel around her.

She stared at herself in the huge mirror over the double basin vanity. Her eyes were darkened by the slight sign of grey circles beneath them, evident from lack of sleep. Gwen searched her reflection, looking for answers to her dilemma. After a moment, she silently cursed herself for not being able to think of a suitable solution. She desperately didn't want to marry David.

Releasing a despairing sigh, she glanced at the floor. Suddenly, she noticed something sparkling to the right of her toes.

It was the engagement ring.

Bending to her knees, Gwen clasped it between her fingers and held it before her. The gold band shone brightly and the magnificent diamond glittered in the fluorescent light. Her gaze narrowed on the ring as thoughts of her situation engulfed her. Then she realized: her solution was staring right at her.

***

Blake had been so surprised by Gwen's optimistic demeanor when she'd snatched his hand and dragged him into the library. He had almost believed David had backed down on his threats. Almost. But Gwen's plan was nearly as impressive.

"Do you think it may be possible?" Her voice was so tentative, yet so hopeful.

While Blake was well aware of his brother's continued love for his ex-wife, he wasn't entirely certain if Michelle still felt the same. They were only recently divorced and had continued to remain amicable, up until Michelle had petitioned to alter their custody arrangements.

Their relationship had always been volatile, at times fiery and hostile, while at others immensely passionate and all-consuming. Their problems had more to do with a similarity of character than any incompatibility. They were both opinionated, pig-headed, conceited narcissists who were too murderously ambitious and disturbingly self-involved to compromise on anything or make time for each other and their family as a whole. It was only after their divorce that something appeared to change in both of them, making Emily and her wellbeing their prime focus.

Blake couldn't be sure if Michelle still loved David. But he was hopeful that Emily's love for her father might prove to be enough to persuade Michelle to give her ex-husband another chance.

Gazing down at Gwen as he held her hands in his, Blake smiled. He wasn't certain her plan would work, but it was definitely worth a try.

"How about we invite Michelle to the New Year's Eve party?"

Gwen frowned, disappointedly. "There's another party?"

He chuckled. "Don't you know the Davenports are famous for their parties?"

"I had hoped it was only necessary for me to survive one."

She had him laughing again. "I promise I'll get you through this next one in a similar fashion to the last," he teased.

He watched as her face blushed at the reminder of their intimate interlude on the balcony.

"Promises, promises," she told him. She planted a brief kiss on his lips. Then she frowned. "Wait, what about Emily? Your brother's idea of a celebration is hardly a place for small children."

Blake nodded. David did have a tendency to create more of an adult atmosphere at his events. "We could persuade him to improve upon that. Surely a party with Emily in attendance would be more of a celebration for him than the sight of numerous naked invitees."

Gwen beamed up at him. "I think you're on to something, Mr. Davenport."

Blake smiled. "Only due to your help, love."

"Here," he told her, making his voice deep with affection. Releasing her left hand for a moment, he snatched the engagement ring from the desktop next to them and gently slipped it on Gwen's finger. She sighed, but obliged him. "I think it best you wear this for the moment. It will help convince David of your continued compliance to his demands." Their gazes met as he did so and in that moment Blake wished the action had been of more significance to both of them.

Maybe one day, the moment would be repeated with a ring and a promise of his own. It was something he was beginning to long for, something he wished he'd been bold and impulsive enough to do before his brother's own deceitful proposal. If only he'd known how quickly things were about to change, he would have made Gwen his in a heartbeat. With all his being, he prayed that he would have another opportunity.

"Perhaps if we both work on him as inconspicuously as possible, you in reference to Emily attending, while I try to convince him to invite Michelle, maybe then we can help him begin to realize that he has a better avenue to pursue."

Gwen's expression remained serious. "It's a great idea, but how will we persuade Michelle to come, once he's open to it?"

Blake smiled at her. "Leave that to me. As soon as we're sure David's keen to have them attend, I can drive down to Brisbane and talk to Michelle."

Gripping his hands tighter in hers, Gwen bit her lip nervously. "I really hope this works."

Blake nodded. "Me, too."

Smiling, she moved to place another soft kiss to his lips, but he quickly stopped her.

"There's just one more thing," he told her.

His heart ached at the thought of what he was about to say.

"Unfortunately, to better convince David, we'll have to keep our distance from each other for a while."

Gwen's happy expression dropped in disappointment.

At the sight, a twinge of pain stung deep in his chest and he quickly wrapped her in a loving embrace.

"I'm not saying we can't be together in the same room,

maybe even steal a few moments like this, but until we've managed to get him to consider inviting Michelle and Emily, we'll have to be very careful around him."

Gwen nodded. "I understand. I just didn't realize how upset I'd be at the idea."

Pulling back slightly so he could gaze into her beautiful green eyes, Blake grinned down at her. "Does that mean you like being with me?"

She smiled coyly. "Maybe just a little."

He sighed contentedly and hugged her closer. "I like being with you, too," he whispered.

At his words, Blake felt her arms tighten affectionately around his back and he realized he didn't ever want to let her go.

"It'll only be for a short while," he told her. But even as he said it, he wondered whom he was trying to convince more, Gwen or himself?

CHAPTER SIXTEEN

Through her dark sunglasses, Gwen watched as Blake climbed free of the pool. She noted his black, opaque swim trunks with slight disappointment. Having escaped the house in her magenta balconette bikini, she had strategically positioned herself on the sun lounge with the best outlook. Unfortunately, enjoying the view a little too much meant she was failing miserably at pretending to read the novel in her hands.

She turned the book the right way up, but continued to gaze over the cover. Blake gave her a saucy grin and headed in her direction. Gwen's heart did an excited little flip-flop at the sight of him approaching. His wet, rippling muscles held her gaze captive before she realized she was in danger of drooling. Quickly, she turned her attention to her book. It was just a shame she now appeared to be reading backward, starting at the end.

She sighed.

It had been two long days since their last embrace, their last kiss, and she was starving for his attention and affection. Gwen knew that he was only keeping his distance to better help their cause, but she hadn't known it would be so dreadfully painful. She yearned to run into his arms, forcing their bodies close while she smothered him in kisses. The thought made her wonder if he felt the same.

She glanced up at him as he reached the end of her sun lounge. Blake stared down at her, his gaze turning dark and lustful as he devoured her figure with his eyes. She couldn't help but smile. At least they were suffering together.

Returning the grin, he sat beside her feet on the lounge. As he leaned back casually, his taut body soaking up the late-morning sun, his fingers crept ever so close to her calves. Gwen's skin prickled with electricity at the sensation of his body so near hers. It was an unbearable kind of torture.

"How are you doing, love?"

"Missing you." The words left her lips before she could think them through. She felt her face blush at her candid response.

Blake gazed down at her, his dark eyes filled with a desire they both shared.

"Miss you, too," he told her.

She sat up slightly, her hand, as if with a mind of its own, reaching for his thigh. Noticing her mistake in time to alter it, she dropped her hand before his, leaving the tips of their fingers mere millimeters from each other. Her fingertips tingled in desperation.

"I miss touching you," she murmured.

He smiled and stretched his hand just slightly. The soft skin of their fingers kissed briefly, sending sparks of electricity up her arm, shadowed by goosebumps.

"You and me both." His voice seemed deepened with desire.

"When will all of this be over?" Despair filled her.

Though they had continued to find moments to disappear to secluded sanctuaries throughout the past two and a half days, Blake had been adamant they do their best to keep things visibly platonic. Neither of them wanted to be caught by David while they were in a compromising embrace, especially if they wanted their plan to succeed.

Unapologetically, Gwen had already broken his rule several times, stealing his hand for an instant just to remind herself of his touch. But their suffering had not been for nothing. Gwen had been successful in getting David to change his party plans to a more child-friendly celebration and had even gained his word that he would be thrilled to have Emily attend. Blake, on the other hand, had not been so lucky. David would not budge on his position to refuse to invite Michelle. It appeared his pride would not allow him to make any kind of amends.

With David standing fast, it seemed they had reached a stalemate. Emily was now invited but Michelle was not and without Michelle, Emily would not attend, and vice-versa. Gwen was beginning to think it was time to move to Plan B. That was, if they actually had a Plan B.

Blake's expression became kind and reassuring. "I'm planning to visit Michelle tomorrow."

Gwen's eyes widened. So they did have a Plan B.

"But tomorrow's the thirtieth. Doesn't David have you booked into a golf game for the morning?"

He nodded. "I'll play perfect brother until I'm no longer needed and then I'll slip away."

All of a sudden, his expression became very serious.

"I'm going to tell her."

Gwen's jaw dropped at his words. "I thought that was a last resort."

With sadness in his eyes, Blake shrugged. "I think we've run out of options, love. I'm hoping that if I tell her what David has planned, she'll either be so jealous that she'll try to win him back, or she'll be so furious that she'll use the knowledge to her advantage in the custody battle, destroying my brother's plan completely."

"Do you really think this will work? I'm afraid if we share the truth, we may find ourselves even further drawn into your brother's relationship drama."

Blake's smile was half-hearted. "Michelle has always been fond of me. I'm sure she'll support us and do everything she can to help solve our dilemma."

Gwen frowned nervously. "I really hope you're right."

His smiled widened. "Of course I am, love." Yet his tone was not as assured as his grin.

Blake seemed to note her concerned expression and he bravely covered her hand with his.

Gwen shivered at the warmth of his skin on hers. Her lust for him had made even the simplest of touches seem sexual, sending enjoyable sensations throughout her body. Her nipples hardened and a pleasurable twinge between her legs had her biting her lip at the thought of where else his hands had been.

As though he could read her thoughts, Blake's dark gaze bore into hers, mirroring her own expression of unbridled yearning.

"If only you knew how much I *want* you, what I *long* to do to you." His words were throaty and pained.

A tingle of pleasure had all the muscles in her groin quivering. Gwen pressed her thighs together against the sensation, licking her lips as she stared hungrily at Blake's mouth.

"And what exactly would that be?" Her voice was husky with desire.

A devilish smile spread across his lips. His hand covering hers rose just enough to allow his fingers to caress her almost secretly.

"If I could have you right now," he told her, his tone seductive, "I would capture those luscious lips with my mouth."

Even as he said it, Gwen found herself moistening her lips with a gentle lick of her tongue. "Yes?" She breathed the word in anticipation.

"And I'd train that naughty, little tongue with my own until I coaxed a small moan from that delicate throat."

Gwen's breath quickened at the thought as he

illustrated his words on the sensitive skin of her hand. Her heartbeat raced at the irresistible feeling.

Blake's gaze narrowed lustfully as he watched her. "I would free you of that flimsy bikini in seconds, as my mouth kissed the smooth nape of your neck." His gaze dropped lower. "Then I'd lavish your perfect breasts with the attention they deserved, devouring your pert nipples, nipping them with my teeth while my hands caressed your supple body."

Gwen felt her chest swell at the thought, her breasts thrusting closer to him, as if to tempt him to give in to his desires. Her insides quivered at the touch of his fingers on her hand as they danced, swirling and gently pinching, in a performance of his words.

"I would roam farther down your body, seeking out your sweetest spot and stroking you there until you were wet with passion and begging for me to be inside you."

A twinge somewhere between pleasure, somewhere between pain, sent little fireworks of sensation through her most precious part and she felt moisture pool between her legs. Gwen pressed her thighs closer and gnawed at her lower lip in an effort to control herself.

Blake's dark and hungry gaze held Gwen's in an ardent stare.

"Then I'd fill you, letting the full size of me enter the warm, moist softness of you. First gently, then harder."

He stroked the back of her hand, slowly up then down. It wasn't difficult for her to imagine the real sensation. Another sensual twinge tugged at her insides.

Gwen tried to control her breathing, to calm her excitement, afraid that if she didn't, she was almost definitely liable to make love to Blake right then and there, outside, for all the world—and David—to see.

"I'd press my body to yours, rocking against you, filling you deeply with each rhythmic thrust." Blake's voice fell an octave lower as he appeared lost, like Gwen, in a world of pleasurable fantasy.

Gwen struggled to catch her breath. Her body was now aching for his. Blake's fingers caressing her skin were no longer enough to satisfy her intense craving for him. She wanted him, wanted his body, and yearned for the ecstasy they could offer each other.

The look in Blake's eyes reflected Gwen's own irrepressible desire and she wondered how much longer he could keep himself under control. A naughty part of her wished he'd throw caution to the wind and just ravish her right there; to hell with David and his threats.

All of a sudden, the click of the French doors opening had Gwen flinching in fright. As Blake followed her gaze to the balcony, Margaret exited the house. Gwen released a breath in a thankful sigh as Blake glanced at her with a brief expression of relief.

Margaret quickly headed over to them. When she reached them, she smiled.

"I hope I'm not interrupting anything, Mr. Davenport. Miss Deveraux." Her tone suggested otherwise, as though her housekeeper-senses had picked up on their flirtatious behavior. After glancing between them almost suspiciously, she focused on Blake.

"Your brother wishes to see you in the study. He desires your help with the new party arrangements."

Blake offered her a smile and nodded. "Sure thing, Margaret. You can tell him I'll be there in a moment."

She nodded and gave them such a knowing expression that it had Gwen expecting her to wink. But then Margaret turned and, without so much as another word, she left the two of them to continue to struggle against their sexual tension.

When Margaret was safely back inside and the balcony door was securely closed, Blake returned his attention to Gwen.

"I should probably go and get changed. Mustn't keep David waiting."

She gave him a half-hearted smile.

He squeezed her hand reassuringly with his own and offered her a brighter smile. "After tomorrow, everything will start to get better, I promise."

"I'm going to hold you to that," she teased.

His grin widened at her playfulness. Then reluctantly, he released her hand and stood up. "Until our next stolen moment together," he told her, lovingly.

Though her expression was full of acknowledgement and understanding, her heart once again ached at his leaving. She hated not knowing when they'd get another moment alone together. Spending time with him, whether in a platonic or sexual context, was her favorite part of the day and was the only thing she seemed to look forward to while trapped in David's mansion-prison.

Blake was quickly becoming the most important person in the world to her and her feelings of distrust had almost completely disappeared. She wondered how she'd ever believed him to be the roguish Davenport brother, how she'd ever given value to those exaggerated magazine articles on his playboy behavior. Blake was nothing like how the media, or David, portrayed him to be. He was a handsome, intelligent, creative man who was full of so much love, affection, and loyalty that it actually surprised her.

His gorgeous smile reassured her once more before he left her side and headed for the pool house.

As Gwen watched him leave, she knew that now, more than anything else, she wanted that wonderful man. She wanted Blake to be hers. She only wished it wasn't too late to make it a reality.

TAMMY MANNERSLY

CHAPTER SEVENTEEN

The repetitive thump-thump of Gwen's feet on the silently whirring treadmill had her entering a trance of concerned thoughts. What if Blake couldn't escape David to go to Brisbane and see Michelle? What if Michelle didn't want to help them? What if their whole plan backfired? Would Gwen really have to marry David?

With the men away at the local golf course for the morning, Gwen had decided to take advantage of the enormous gymnasium at her disposal. The mansion's gym was equipped with the most modern exercise machines and every new piece of tele-marketed, fad-inducing equipment in the fitness industry. Though Gwen was no longer much of a runner, having given up running track and competitive swimming after high school, she still considered both sports an enjoyable pastime. As solo activities, they also gave her the opportunity to gather and work through her thoughts, especially when faced with a difficult dilemma.

Being so uncertain about her impending future, Gwen couldn't help but feel fearful about what would happen on New Year's Eve. The party was just over twenty-four hours away and nothing of their plan had been finalized.

David was set and prepared for Emily to attend, having changed his plans and arranged a more child-friendly celebration, but had yet to actually invite her. Perhaps he was hoping his brother would perform the difficult task of asking Michelle's consent, rather than forcing him to put aside his own pride. Even then there was no guarantee.

David had been so quick and hospitable to alter his party plans, as though very eager to have his daughter attend. Yet it seemed that he'd rather be prepared and hopeful for her arrival rather than actually have the courage to assure her attendance through personal invitation. Gwen couldn't quite understand his actions. Surely with such excitement about the new celebration, he would have been even more keen to ensure his daughter would come. Things just didn't seem to make sense. But maybe David was playing a larger game than she realized, with Blake and her falling into the roles he'd already assumed for them? How could she possibly know what he had planned?

With a touch of a button, she quickened her pace, finding the stress on her limbs a relief for her anxiety. She ran faster and faster, holding the intensity for a few minutes until she felt the euphoric burst of endorphins wash over her. Her chest felt lighter and her limbs tingled with a feeling somewhere between exhaustion and pleasure. Slowing to a walk, she began to stretch her muscles with each step, calming their tension and relieving their exertion. Minutes passed and her body had relaxed substantially. Switching off the machine, she jumped down to the floor and turned around.

Her eyes met Blake's across the room and she gasped.

"You scared me," she giggled. She grabbed one of the towels provided on a rack beside the treadmills and headed over to him.

He stood by the door to the hall, casually leaning against the frame as he watched her. At her words, a smirk crossed his lips.

"Sorry, love. But when you didn't hear me open the door, I thought it best not to disturb you."

She smiled suspiciously at him. "Oh, what a gentleman," she teased. "I'm sure the view of everything *bouncing* around didn't inform your decision much, either?" Gwen motioned to her curves squeezed into the small crop top and tight bike pants that were her gym attire.

Blake chuckled. "What can I say? I'm an opportunistic man."

Gwen smirked and rolled her eyes. "Have you been perving long?"

"Cheeky," he chided her. Blake shook his head and pushed himself free of the wall. "I only just got home. Strangely enough, David sent me back early. Apparently, he wants me to drive to Brisbane and pick up Emily."

Gwen's eyes widened in surprise. "So he's asked Michelle, then? She's consented to Emily coming to the New Year's Eve party?"

Blake frowned. "Not quite. I'm being sent to ask for both Michelle's consent, God knows how long that will take, and then to drive Emily back up the coast."

With a sigh, Gwen felt her expression fall in disappointment. "So what's the plan?"

He shrugged. "Nothing's changed. I'm going ahead as we discussed. I'm still hoping that when Michelle learns the truth, she will help us out of our predicament."

"We're really putting all our eggs in one basket with this one, aren't we?" Gwen gnawed at her lower lip in worry.

"That's one way of looking at it, love, but I'm trying to remain positive. We are short of options as it is. To not at least give it a shot would be to waste a good opportunity."

"And you're an *opportunistic* man." Gwen smiled.

"Exactly." Blake's expression mirrored hers.

"So, when are you leaving?" Gwen didn't realize how sad she'd feel until the words left her lips. She didn't want Blake to disappear down to Brisbane without her. Who knew how long he'd be gone?

"In a few minutes." He sounded almost as forlorn as she did. "I just have to gather a few things and change out of these clothes."

Gwen glanced down at the grass stains on his beige slacks. "I didn't realize the green fought back," she said playfully.

Blake chuckled and shook his head. "While my brother may be a brilliant golfer and I know vaguely which direction to hit the ball, David's friends aren't so skilled. It's a dangerous sport, really. Divots were flying everywhere."

He had Gwen laughing. "I'd pay to see that," she told him.

His smile grew larger and he opened his arms out to her. "You should feel sorry for me," he teased. "How about a sympathetic hug?"

Gwen's face brightened and she almost jumped on him in excitement. For days now, she had been waiting to embrace him properly. Finally, with David out of the house, she had her chance. But she stopped and glanced down at herself.

"But I'm all sweaty and disgusting." Her voice was disheartened.

"You're beautiful as always." Blake grinned at her. "Besides, what's a little sweat between lovers?"

Snatching her hand, he pulled her close and dropped her into a dip over his knee. Gwen could barely catch her breath, she was so astonished. Blake's handsome face smiled down at her, all dark features and seductive twinkle, before his mouth captured hers.

The softness of his lips caressed the silky skin of her own, while his hands lustfully grasped the curves of her body. Then, as quickly as it had begun, their embrace ended and Blake was steadying her back on her feet.

"I wish I didn't have to leave," he told her. His hands still refusing to release hers.

"You could always take me with you." Even as she said it in her super-sweet tone, Gwen already knew his answer.

If David arrived home and she wasn't there, she doubted he would understand her desire for a sudden road trip. Especially with Blake. No, if she went along, she would surely be kissing her career goodbye.

With furrowed brows, Blake opened his mouth to answer, but Gwen quickly shushed him with a finger to his lips.

"I know," she told him. "It's okay. I just wish I could stay with you, but I understand the difficulty of our circumstances."

He pulled her closer, slipping his arms affectionately behind her back. His dark eyes held her gaze, soul-searching, while his hands held her soft body against his.

"If I didn't believe that I could save you by leaving, I never would. But, love, I really do believe we have a chance once Michelle learns the truth."

Gwen nodded. While she believed that Blake believed he was doing the right thing, she still didn't feel entirely certain. Nevertheless, she appreciated the fact he kept endeavoring to put her mind at ease. Over the past few days, she had grown to trust and value his judgment, more than she once ever believed she could. Knowing him the way she did now, she trusted that he had her best interests at heart and that he would do all he could to help free her from the confines of his brother's blackmail. Yet in not knowing Michelle personally and having only heard of her many similarities to David, Gwen could not disregard her rational fear that Michelle might, in turn, decide to play her own games with them.

"I trust you," Gwen told him.

At her words, Blake's eyes lit up and he pressed a brief but passionate kiss to her lips.

"You really mean that?" His tone seemed overwhelmed and excited.

She smiled up at him. "Of course I do."

He breathed a contented sigh. "You don't know how much that means to me."

Seeing his reaction, her face brightened. "I think I do."

Gwen thought back to a few days before, when she wouldn't have trusted Blake with an errand, let alone something as important as her future wellbeing. It embarrassed her now to think of how poorly she'd thought of him and how harshly she'd judged him. Yet he had persisted, had done his best to prove his worth to her, to prove he could be trusted.

"You have more than earned my trust, Blake. Now that I know you so much better, I am ashamed of how I treated you before."

"Don't be, love," he told her. He hugged her tightly, resting his head lightly atop hers. "My past mistakes led to my poor reputation, so you had every right to suspect me of what you had heard I was capable of. I am just glad we have moved past that."

Gwen sighed into the warmth of his chest. "I just wish we could move further."

"Patience, love." He chuckled softly. "If all goes well in Brisbane, I may be able to keep *my promises* sooner."

Gwen's body reacted with a burst of pleasurable tingles at the mere thought of what he'd promised was yet to come.

"Let's hope so," she told him with a grin.

She relaxed into the hard lines of his body, cuddling him close and wishing they could stay that way—in each other's arms—forever. While she knew he would have to break their embrace eventually, to prepare for his quest to the city, she was sure they had a few more seconds of utter bliss and contentment to share.

Though stealing secret seconds together would never be enough to satisfy her desire for him. She was now much too lost in love for that.

CHAPTER EIGHTEEN

Blake drove David's black Porsche down the highway. He had at least another hour of traveling time before he reached Michelle's. He wished David had the decency to call ahead, or at least allow him to pay Michelle the same common courtesy. But no, his brother would remain stubborn until the end. Apparently, in his mind, Michelle no longer deserved that kind of consideration. She'd started their "war" by initiating the custody battle, therefore she'd forfeited any right she had to be treated amicably. Or at least, that was what David thought.

Blake couldn't believe he'd willingly chosen to squeeze himself further between the two of them. If it hadn't been the only way he felt certain he could save the livelihood and future happiness of the woman he loved, then he would be miles away from the both of them. But, as it was, he was on his way to make peace with the banshee in the hope of encouraging her to give the beast a second chance. In truth, David and Michelle were perfect for each other—at least in a dysfunctional fairytale sort of way—but their controlling personalities and inflated egos had ruined their initial opportunity for a lasting marriage. Blake hoped he stood any chance of helping them reconcile.

"You have to do your best for Gwen." The quiet words left his lips like a mantra.

Of course, he would do everything in his power to rescue Gwen from his brother's devilish scheme. There was no way he would allow her to walk down the aisle and marry someone she didn't love, and who didn't love her. That was not an option anymore. He would not abandon her to the fate she faced with David or the future she would be dealt if she crossed him.

He had come to love Gwen so fervently, so whole-heartedly with all his being, that he could not imagine living a life without her in it. She was everything he'd ever desired, everything in a loving wife that he'd ever searched for. Yet he never believed such a woman could exist, until he'd met her. She was kind-hearted, considerate, honest, and passionate. She was caring, affectionate, creative, and virtuous. Gwen had a strong will that mirrored Blake's own tenacity and an unbreakable loyalty to all those she cared for. She strived to think the best of everyone, even taking kindly to him when she'd believed his roguish reputation. Just being around Gwen made Blake feel like the man he aspired to be, and inspired him to do better. And best of all, he believed she loved him as he loved her. What more could he want?

Gwen Deveraux was the woman of his dreams and now that Blake had found her, he wanted to be with her always and forever. He just prayed she felt the same.

***

Gwen sat at the dining room table, waiting for David. Margaret had told her that dinner was ready to be served, but that was a little over twenty minutes ago. While Gwen didn't mind prolonging the awkwardness that would surely come about during a dinner with only her and David in attendance, her stomach was beginning to eat itself.

She tapped her fingers quietly on the empty place

setting in front of her and thought back to earlier in the day. Even with the heavy anvil of David's blackmail hanging over her head, her day had been bearable. She had finally been able to once again embrace the man she loved, without fear of the consequences. Blake had hugged her, kissed her, and reminded her why she craved his loving affection so desperately. In his arms, Gwen felt enraptured, she felt loved, and, more than anything else, she felt like the woman she desired to be. His belief and love for her seemed to encourage her own belief in herself, and when he was with her, she believed she could accomplish anything.

Gwen sighed. Her heart ached at the distance between them. Rationally, she understood why Blake had to go to Brisbane, but romantically, she wished she could be by his side, to face the world with all its difficulties and possibilities. Together they could achieve anything, she was certain of that.

The thud of a footstep entering the dining room brought her thoughts back to her current, difficult situation.

David nodded at Gwen in greeting as he took his seat beside her at the head of the table.

Once he'd arrived, Margaret didn't waste any time serving their dinner. Bowls of hot pasta were placed before them, while a dish of salad and a plate of bread rolls were placed in the center. She opened a bottle of Cabernet Sauvignon and placed it beside David, knowing too well that he enjoyed pouring his own. Then, once she'd performed her role, Margaret left the room without a word.

David poised the bottle above Gwen's glass. "Wine?"

It was the first word he'd spoken to her in almost a day. Whether his conscience, if he even had one, was actually getting the better of him, or if he just couldn't be bothered wasting the time or energy conversing with her, Gwen didn't know. Either way, she had found the silence more than tolerable, especially when she was struggling not to yell at him each rare time they were alone together.

She nodded. "Yes, thank you." Perhaps the wine would take the edge off their awkward dinner together.

David poured her a glass and then filled his own. As he took a sip, she felt his eyes watching her.

Gwen glanced up at him, her hand covering her mouth as she chewed a large mouthful of Margaret's delicious pasta.

David just sat there staring at her, looking rather pleased with himself as he sipped his wine. His expression resembled that of a movie villain. All he needed to complete the picture was the fluffy cat on his lap.

If Gwen didn't know better, she would wonder if the food was poisoned. But surely, even he wasn't capable of something like that, especially when it would only hinder the outcome of his evil plan.

When she was able to swallow, she questioned him. "You're in a good mood this evening. Did you have a good time at golf?"

He smiled. "I always have a good time when I win."

Gwen forced herself not to roll her eyes at his egotistical statement and continued eating her dinner.

"I'm not ignorant, Gwen. I know what you and my brother have planned."

She paused mid-mouthful, almost choking on her food. Looking up at him, her expression full of shock, she swallowed painfully.

"W-what do you mean?"

His expression turned stern. "I don't appreciate your coyness, Gwen."

His seriousness had her convinced there was no point in lying. Obviously, somehow, he had found out that Blake was going to tell Michelle about the blackmail.

"You're the one who sent him to Brisbane, David. How can you expect him to visit Michelle and not disclose what you've been up to recently?"

A sly smile twisted his lips. "I knew he couldn't resist telling her." Even David's tone began to resemble that of a B-movie villain.

Gwen felt her face contort in disgust. Just who did David think he was? If he didn't consider blackmail something to be ashamed of, then perhaps there was nothing that could shame him.

"Aren't you even a little concerned about what your ex-wife will think of you once she knows the truth?" Gwen had to ask, but she felt as though she already knew the answer.

"No. Of course not." He almost laughed. "Michelle knew who I was when she married me. She knows what I'm capable of and how far I'd be willing to go to get what I want, just as I know that she would do anything to achieve a win."

Gwen forced herself to shut her gaping mouth. Clearly this man had no limits. Then, as if lightning had stuck, she realized something.

"You said you knew Blake couldn't resist telling Michelle?" She posed it as a question while she gathered her thoughts.

David just smiled his cunning smile.

The truth hit her like a mental bombshell. "You wanted this to happen? You gave us no other choice except to talk to Michelle. This was part of your plan from the beginning." Gwen couldn't hide the anger from her voice.

How dare he use her and Blake so heartlessly, moving them around his own little chessboard like traumatized pawns! He had cornered them both into a difficult situation, forcing them to involve themselves in his family affairs, probably so that he didn't have to.

With a simple nod, David confirmed Gwen's terrible realization.

"What are you hoping to achieve by all of this?" She growled her words through clenched teeth.

His grin was suddenly more sincere. "I want Michelle

and Emily to come home." Even his tone sounded genuinely hopeful.

Gwen found herself bewildered by his confession. She almost felt sorry for him. "But this isn't their home anymore, David."

He gave her a condescending glare. "I'm optimistic, not imbecilic, Miss Deveraux."

She frowned at him. At least his sudden rudeness proved he wasn't in danger of losing his grip on reality.

"Once Michelle learns of my behavior, she'll have to return here to reproach me. She's not one to shy away from a fight or a chance to lay blame."

Gwen still felt puzzled by the whole situation. "So, you're saying that you forced Blake into a position where he felt it necessary to inform your ex-wife of your criminal behavior, which would in turn send her back to you, if only briefly and for the wrong reasons?" She said her words slowly, as if trying to understand them better once verbalized.

David nodded. "That's the gist of it. Yes. But Gwen, there is much more to it than that."

While she tried to remove the grimace she felt her face form at his admittance of absolute insanity, she pushed her bowl of food away. At all this talk of sickeningly ridiculous games, Gwen no longer had an appetite.

Examining her carefully, David sat up and rested his elbows on the table.

"What you don't understand, Gwen, is that things would never have worked out the same way if I had approached Michelle. Stubborn as we both are, the chance of that even occurring, without one of us suffering a personality alteration, is highly unlikely." His expression became almost apologetic. "I couldn't fathom another way of achieving my goal. I know Blake has strong morals and I depended on them in making this whole situation come to pass."

Anger and confusion clouded Gwen's thoughts. David

had basically just admitted that he had dragged her and Blake into his relationship drama because he didn't have the courage or the humility to talk to his ex-wife himself. She shook her head in disbelief.

"Does that mean the whole blackmail debacle was just for show? To scare us into doing your bidding?"

David laughed in her face. "Oh no. Not at all. I meant every word. The future of your teaching career is in my hands until I win my case in the custody suit or until Michelle forfeits and puts an end to this ridiculous farce."

"But surely you can't still expect me to agree to this marriage?" She displayed her hand to him as if the jewelry on her finger disgusted her.

He shrugged. "If all goes to plan, there will be no need. If not, then our union can still assist my goal."

Gwen was outraged. "You would hold me to this? Even though I know the truth? Even though you're aware your own brother has feelings for me?"

David frowned. "Yes. That's a pity. Unfortunately, that was never part of my plan. It was pure coincidence. Yet it was beneficial, at least in encouraging Blake to confess all to Michelle." He narrowed his gaze. "He really wants to do all he can to rescue you from my clutches, doesn't he?"

Seeing Gwen's scowl, David laughed and leaned back in his chair.

"I'm really not as evil as the two of you seem to think." His tone was too jovial.

Fury flared within Gwen at David's mockery. Of course he was evil. Maybe he should take a long look in the mirror. Or a long walk on a short pier. She was tired of being at his will, of playing his game by his rules. As soon as she could leave the room, she'd call Blake and fill him in on the extent of his brother's schemes.

David's expression became serious as he watched Gwen's anger furrow her brow.

"I am not evil, Gwen. I am just a man who is used to getting what he wants, at any cost. And when it comes to my daughter, no one and nothing can keep me from her. I hope, if nothing else, you understand that."

Gwen felt herself sympathize with him and then immediately, she regretted it. She could comprehend what he meant: if she had a child of her own, she would do almost anything to ensure she remained in their life. But at the cost of the welfare and happiness of others innocent to her cause? No, she would never stoop *that* low. David was alone in his choice to affect her life and that of his brother. He was the one who was causing them pain emotionally, even physically, not Michelle or her child custody lawsuit. It was David's fault she'd had to keep her distance from Blake over the last few days and he was to blame for separating them now.

Her anger returned, flaring so intensely that she could no longer contain it. Gwen pointed an index finger at David in accusation. She could feel her teacher voice demanding to be set free.

"You cannot hide your transgressions behind the guise of protecting your daughter or living up to your fatherly duty. It is time you took responsibility for your actions, David, whether they be morally righteous or downright criminal."

David's eyes widened at Gwen's scolding, as though he hadn't realized she could have such a fiery tone or passionate opinion.

"Though you ignore it, this custody battle has as much to do with you as it does Michelle. For if there were no problems in your relationship, there would be no lawsuit and there would have been no divorce. Michelle and the other people in your life are not solely responsible for your hardships or losses. You, too, have played your own part. And though you deny it, your choices, your plans and schemes, every game you set into motion, has consequences that affect others: some you love, some you barely know. These consequences cause their own reactions, most of which will come back around to affect you in some way or another. These, in turn, create more difficulties for you, more hardships that you have to plan and scheme away in a never-ending circle of hostility and blame."

Gwen stood up abruptly. She'd had just about enough of David's company for one night.

David just watched her, silent and wide-eyed, as if actually hearing her for the first time since she'd arrived at his home.

"When are you going to start realizing, David, that you are just as responsible for your failures as you are your successes? When will you understand that by having no limits and by putting everything into the win, you are ultimately losing everything to the win? Winning and success are not the legendary glories they claim to be without the love, support, and devotion of your family and friends. If you're not careful, you could lose everything. Your brother, your ex-wife, even your daughter. Heed my words, David Davenport. If you keep pushing those you care about, one day you'll push too hard and then you'll have no one left to play your games."

Having had her opportunity to vent, her authoritarian teacher voice now satisfied, Gwen moved to storm out of the room. At that moment, she didn't care if David understood anything she'd said or not. She didn't care if he'd decided to change his ways or if he had even been listening to her. Gwen had had enough of him and his stupid antics. All she wanted to do now was to call Blake and warn him of the extent of his brother's plan.

Yet as she moved, David's voice trailed after her.

"Well, Miss Deveraux, you do have some spunk after all. Who would have thought it?" David's words were almost congratulatory as he spoke them more to the room than to her.

His smart comment was enough for Gwen to shoot him with a furious glare, though not enough to stop her in her mission. She was leaving that room and as soon as it was possible, she was leaving that house. Blake might have been the love of her life, but his brother had only brought her misery and the sooner she could get away from him and his games of manipulation, the better.

But as Gwen reached the door, Margaret rushed into the dining room. Her face was flushed as though she'd hurried and her kind eyes were filled with fear and concern.

Margaret nodded to Gwen as she entered the room in front of her. "Miss Deveraux." Then the housekeeper's worried gaze passed to David.

Gwen's heart lurched as she watched and waited for what she dreaded was about to be bad news.

"Mr. Davenport, please...the phone." Margaret couldn't get the words out.

Her eyes began to glisten with coming tears and she shook her head as if trying, but failing to compose herself. She hurried to his side, placing a hand on his shoulder as she stared down at him with concern.

"David," she whispered. "It's Emily."

CHAPTER NINETEEN

The hospital hallways spread out like a maze before them. The unnatural glow of the fluorescent lights, the similarities of every room, and the jumble of electronically tinged words mumbled through the PA system all sought to disorient them. But nothing would slow David in his search for his daughter.

Gwen struggled to keep up with him as he rushed away in front of her, his stride long and so determined in his mission. Finally they reached another nurses' station. David threw himself at the counter.

"Davenport, Emily. Which room?" Though it was a demand, his tone was filled with such desperation that it was almost heart-wrenching.

Having seen many relatives of patients in a similar state, the young nurse didn't hesitate to offer him the information he required, once he'd provided appropriate identification.

"Emily Davenport is in a private room. Two-twenty-four. Down that hall, fourth room on your right." With an elegantly manicured finger, she pointed them in the right direction.

"Thank you," Gwen told her, as David sped away

without so much as a nod in appreciation for her efforts.

Gwen hurried after him.

They had driven in silence most of the way down to Brisbane. David had been serious and stoic as he drove, while Gwen had tried to steer her thoughts away from the fear of what might have happened to Emily. Like all her beloved students, that little girl meant the world to her and she couldn't bear to imagine her hurt.

David hadn't exactly asked Gwen to accompany him on the journey. "*Coming?*" was not quite the request for support she had expected. But Gwen could tell that he appreciated her being there. He'd even opened the car door for her when they'd left the house and when they'd arrived at the hospital. It was almost enough to make her question his devilish nature. Yet good manners were not proof of a good heart and Gwen had no intention of forgiving him so easily for his transgressions.

As she watched David hasten down the hall, Gwen knew that none of that mattered right now. He could have been the worst person on earth, but with his child injured—a child they all cared for—all of the troubles between them would be momentarily set aside. The only thing that mattered in this instant was Emily and her wellbeing.

David turned to head into a room just as Blake was making his way out. They shared a few quiet words and David patted Blake on the shoulder as if in gratitude. After watching David disappear into the room, Blake's gaze met Gwen's. When she reached him, his handsome mouth curled in a comforted smile.

"It's good to see you, love."

Before she could say a word, he swept her up into his arms and cuddled her close. Her body relaxed into the warmth of his embrace, her eyes closed, and she sighed. Everything seemed all right when she was with him, when she was wrapped up and protected in his loving hug. All of her problems seemed to vanish and she felt she could lose herself there, but she knew it wasn't reality.

Reluctantly, she opened her eyes and pushed free of him, just enough to see his face.

"Is Emily okay? What happened?" She couldn't hide the fear from her voice.

It was Blake's turn to sigh. "She was at a playdate with friends when she fell off the monkey bars."

Gwen frowned in understanding. It was a common occurrence on the playground at her school, but the bark beneath usually cushioned the fall enough for the child to avoid injury. She wished Emily had been so lucky.

"Is she badly hurt?"

Blake shook his head. "The doctor says she has a sprained wrist. Her body weight fell on it as she landed. But from what I understand, she was at the end of the course, so as she fell, she also hit her head against the step."

Gwen cringed at the thought. That would have been a painful fall.

"Poor Emily." The words left her lips in breathy worry.

Blake rubbed Gwen's shoulders reassuringly.

"It's okay. She has a slight bruise on her forehead, which may blossom into quite a shiner, but the CT scan was clear. At Michelle's insistence, the doctor has decided to keep Emily here overnight in case of concussion."

Gwen raised her eyebrows. "At Michelle's insistence?"

Blake chuckled softly. "She can be very persuasive, as I'm sure you can imagine."

With a smile, Gwen nodded knowingly. Like David, Michelle was obviously one of the rich and powerful who didn't take kindly to being told no.

"I'm surprised she hasn't decided to sue the owners of the play equipment."

"Oh, don't get me started on that," Blake scoffed humorously. "I've just spent the good part of an hour convincing her that suing is not the answer."

Gwen giggled. She hoped he was joking, but knew the

reality was sure to be sillier than the truth.

With a glance inside the room, Blake smiled. "At least it seems something positive has come out of all this."

She gave him a puzzled expression. Emily was injured. Michelle was threatening to sue. She was still being blackmailed by his brother. Just what exactly was the "something positive"?

Gently ushering Gwen to the window in front of Emily's hospital room, Blake glanced through the glass. She followed his gaze.

Little Emily appeared tiny as she slept in the huge hospital bed. Her right wrist was wrapped in a bandage and propped up on a pillow. A linear bruise above her right eye stood out on her pale skin. She looked like an injured porcelain doll as her parents sat by her bedside, their lips moving silently as they shared indistinguishable whispers.

Gwen watched as David wrapped an arm around Michelle's shoulders and she leaned into his embrace.

She felt herself nod. "Oh, *that* something positive," Gwen muttered.

Blake smiled down at her. "I haven't seen them hug in over a year."

As she watched them interact, their fierce love for their daughter obviously breaking down the walls their divorce had built, Gwen could see that David and Michelle were two of a kind. If she didn't know better, didn't know their history, she would have believed they belonged together. The thought made her dare to hope that maybe, just maybe, out of this terrifying accident their relationship could find the strength to improve.

Blake's hand at her waist, hugged her closer. "Seeing this, it would be easy for anyone to mistake them for a loving couple."

Gwen nodded. She gave Blake a small smile. "Let's hope they can realize that and do something about it, before I'm forced to marry your brother."

Blake chuckled and rested his head affectionately atop hers. "I won't let it come to that, love."

He sounded so sure of it that Gwen almost believed him. But he didn't yet know what she did—that David was aware of and controlling almost everything, and that only an end to the custody lawsuit and a reconciliation with Michelle could ensure she wouldn't be walking down the aisle.

As she gazed in on the seemingly adoring couple embracing by their daughter's hospital bed, Gwen said a little prayer that this time, love really would conquer all.

Gwen had never had vending machine coffee before and she was beginning to wish she hadn't offered to fetch some. She was certain the others would find it equally repulsive.

When she paused beside a trash can to throw her cup away, she considered throwing in the tray with the other three. She was quick to think better of it though, realizing that coming back with something was better than facing Emily's vicious parents empty-handed. As it was, they already seemed as though they were on the warpath, ready to pounce on anyone not obliging their exact demands. They had requested the coffee and they were aware the cafeteria was closed for the evening, so their only option had been the vending machine. Surely with that reasoning they couldn't pass her the blame.

As she neared Emily's hospital room, Gwen noticed Michelle standing outside, looking in through the room's window as she and Blake had done earlier. With her perfectly styled golden locks, her faultless makeup and her designer ensemble, Michelle looked as though she belonged in the fashion pages of a magazine, not in a hospital hallway. She appeared distracted by what she was watching and there was a small smile on her face. It was the first pleasant expression Gwen had witnessed on

Michelle.

Mustering her courage, Gwen approached her.

"Coffee?" With a smile, she held out the tray.

Michelle's eyes fluttered as if waking from a dream and her stern expression returned when she laid her eyes on Gwen.

"I should warn you it's not very good coffee." Gwen attempted small talk, doing her best to be friendly.

"I don't really care if it's sludge," Michelle told her. Her tone remained as hostile as in their brief first encounter. "Just as long as it contains caffeine."

She snatched out a cup and then continued to stare into the room.

Gwen followed her gaze.

Blake was on one side of the hospital bed, holding Emily's hand comfortingly, while David sat on the other stroking his daughter's white-blond curls off her forehead.

Gwen couldn't help but smile at the sight of two strong, alpha males reduced to mere emotional saps in the company of an injured child. Even after all she'd been through over the past few days, Gwen still found it adorable.

"I hope you want children."

Michelle's blunt statement caught Gwen off guard.

"Pardon me?"

Crossing her arms almost aggressively over her chest, Michelle turned to face her. She was easily Gwen's height in her expensive high heels and she used every inch she could to create a stance of dominance.

"Blake wants to have children."

Gwen still found herself flabbergasted. While she loved the fact that she and Blake had that in common, she didn't understand how it was of relevance to the situation. Feeling certain that a sarcastic remark, such as "does he now" or "that's nice", might antagonize Michelle to the point of suddenly wanting to sue her, Gwen decided silence was her best option.

"Blake is a great man. He is a wonderful uncle and one day, when he is a father, he will excel at that as well."

Gwen felt herself nod at Michelle's stating of the obvious. Luckily, just in time, she managed to stop herself from rolling her eyes before they, too, had an opportunity to offend.

"I support him in everything he does. I care for him as if he is my own brother."

Confused as to Michelle's point, Gwen remained patient and polite.

"In saying all of this, I would expect his partner in life to recognize his greatness and be able to offer him everything and more in a loving, permanent relationship."

Like a light bulb illuminating, the purpose of Michelle's stern rant suddenly became clear. Gwen was receiving the "if you hurt someone I love, I'll destroy you" speech. She had never expected that, of all things, to come from Michelle. In fact, she had never expected to get one in reference to Blake at all. Surely he was big enough and handsome enough to look after himself.

Michelle just stared at her. Apparently, Blake's ex-sister-in-law now required a response.

Gwen offered her a smile in an effort to relieve the obvious tension. "I understand what you're saying, Michelle. Blake deserves the best."

Though Gwen couldn't be sure if she could claim to be the best woman for Blake, she had given Michelle an honest answer.

Over the past few days spent in his company, Gwen had realized that Blake, bad reputation and all, was actually one of the good guys. Though she might have misjudged him initially, she could now see how wonderful he truly was. Just another glance at him in the hospital room, comforting and caring for his little niece, was enough to prove his exceptional qualities far outweighed any poor past behavior. If she hadn't known him personally, hadn't known for certain that he really existed, she would have thought him a fantasy. After all, he was quickly becoming the man of her dreams.

Michelle stared her down. "Do you really understand, Gwen? I'm not sure you do. Blake has never before let a woman touch his heart."

She paused briefly, as if hoping to let her words sink in, eyeing Gwen carefully as she did so.

"And yet here you are, proving there is a first for everything."

Gwen frowned at Michelle's condescending tone, but tried her best not to be offended. Blake had warned her that Michelle could be prickly. Gwen just hadn't realized how much her personal life would come under scrutiny, especially now she and Blake were so close.

Michelle's posture relaxed slightly and she dropped a hand to her hip.

"When Blake came to see me today, I had never seen him so happy and so equally full of concern. For once in his life, he appeared to be passionate about something other than his photography and his philanthropy. It was then that he told me about you."

Gwen felt her face flush with warmth. She was both embarrassed and thrilled. It still hadn't been obvious to her that Blake's feelings were so serious and so sincere. Though Gwen had hoped as much, it had scared her to believe so whole-heartedly, in case she might have been wrong. But, with Michelle's admission, she now knew better.

"Blake loves me?" Gwen's breathy question was met in unison with a statement from Michelle.

"Blake's in love with you."

Gwen's eyes widened in amazement. If rude, snippy, critical Michelle believed as much, then it had to be true. Blake was in love with her, just as Gwen was in love with him. It wasn't just a fantasy, it wasn't just a fling: they really had created a lasting bond. She was suddenly lost for words.

Michelle's gaze narrowed. "Now that it appears we're both on the same page, I feel obliged to warn you. If you hurt my wonderful ex-brother-in-law, I will ensure that you'll never work as a teacher again, in any capacity."

Gwen's jaw dropped and, before she could catch it, she felt herself scoff at Michelle's threat.

Michelle scowled. "Do we have a problem?"

Gwen shook her head. "No, sorry. It's just—"

But she had to stop herself before she verbally noted the similarity. She wasn't sure if Blake had already had an opportunity to tell Michelle about David's blackmail. From their closeness earlier on, Gwen doubted that Michelle was even slightly aware of the devilish plan her ex-husband had set in place. Surely, if she had been, she wouldn't have cuddled up to him so quickly.

"It's just what? I would appreciate it if you finished your sentences."

Gwen swallowed. She didn't want to be the one to break the news, especially not at a time as sensitive as this. But what could she possibly say?

Just as Gwen was wracking her brain for an appropriate lie, Michelle's stern expression softened and she actually laughed.

"Don't worry yourself, Gwen. I know what you were about to say. It's just that my ex-husband made the same threat to you recently, or something along those lines. I know all about it. Blake filled me in as soon as he arrived. It's also incredibly difficult to miss that ring."

Gwen shook her head in disbelief. How could Michelle be so cheerful if she actually knew the truth? Her ex was blackmailing her daughter's teacher into marrying him. Gwen couldn't see the funny side.

"And you're okay with everything? You don't notice the problem here?"

Michelle's expression lit up, as though she'd just realized she'd missed something.

"Oh, sorry. I should apologize for my poor sense of

humor. I was joking before. Of course I wouldn't ruin your career. If you really did hurt my Blake, I could do much worse."

For just a moment, Michelle's voice slipped back into its threatening tone and Gwen found herself slightly terrified as to what horrors Michelle might have been referring to.

Yet one look at Gwen's fearful expression seemed enough to return the kind lilt and Michelle was back on course, explaining her point.

"And of course I think it highly inappropriate of my ex-husband to be blackmailing you into marriage, though I doubt he ever considered it would go that far. I'm sure all of his threats were more for my benefit than anything else. He always did like to make me jealous. Both that, and infuriate me. In this instance, he has achieved both."

A smile crossed Michelle's face at the thought. It was enough to make Gwen wonder at the stability of her sanity. How could she possibly enjoy being manipulated into feeling jealousy and fury? Especially by her ex? Clearly, the relationship David and Michelle shared was beyond anything Gwen had ever known, or ever wished to know. As far as she was concerned, she just wanted them to keep their unusual behavior to themselves and leave her out of their volatile relationship.

"So, does this mean you will help us? You'll put an end to the custody battle and free me of my obligation to David?"

Gwen hated that her tone had sounded so hopeful. She didn't yet trust Michelle and she was sure that it would be in her best interest not to, until she had proof otherwise.

Michelle made a tsk-tsk noise with her tongue. "It's not really as simple as all that, Gwen. Of course, you can ignore the blackmail. If David takes it that far, which I'm certain he won't, I'll fight him on everything. There's also no way I'll allow *you* to marry my ex-husband."

Gwen frowned. While she was relieved, nearly elated at

hearing she was protected from the threat of blackmail, she didn't understand Michelle's emphasis on her as though she was the problem. Wasn't it the other way around? And why on earth would she want to be *allowed* to marry David? Clearly, Michelle had suffered from a Freudian slip of jealousy.

"But when it comes to the custody lawsuit," Michelle continued, "only David can encourage me to call off the legal hounds."

Narrowing her gaze, Gwen nodded. "Okay, I can understand that. David needs to make amends before you can return to a more amicable relationship."

Michelle gave her a curt nod. "Precisely."

Pulling together a little courage, Gwen smiled and asked Michelle what she had been thinking since seeing her embrace David in Emily's hospital room. "When I saw you together earlier, I thought things might have improved between you. In fact, if I hadn't known otherwise, I would have believed that you still loved him."

Michelle opened her mouth to retort, but stopped and seemed to mull over Gwen's words for a moment.

She gazed into Emily's room once more. Her daughter's eyelids fluttered awake briefly as she stared up at her father and offered him a sleepy smile. David pressed a gentle kiss to her cheek and Emily's eyes closed once more. Michelle's face lit up lovingly at the sight. Turning back to Gwen, she shrugged almost helplessly.

"Sometimes our concern for that which we both hold most precious in the world will always find a way to bring us closer together."

With a nod, Gwen smiled. "Sometimes it's *the love* we hold for each other, whether declared or denied, that will always bring us closer together in a time of need."

A wide grin spread across Michelle's lips as though a secret had suddenly been discovered. "Touché, Gwen," she told her. "You may just be a perfect match for my Blake, after all."

And in that moment everything finally seemed to make sense. Gwen wondered how she hadn't noticed it earlier, since it seemed so obvious now. Michelle was still in love with David, just as he was still in love with her.

Though Michelle worked hard to publicly renounce the idea that she could still be in love with him, she clearly protested too much. The custody battle was never about forcing David to make amends: it was about encouraging him to fight for their love. Though she may have been going about it the wrong way, Michelle was giving their love for each other a final chance to conquer all—at the risk of it being snuffed out forever.

CHAPTER TWENTY

Blake opened the dark oak front door and ushered Gwen back into the Davenport mansion.

Though he had been prepared to stay overnight in the city, in case his brother or Michelle needed help with Emily, David had told him that he would be of more assistance back up the coast. Apparently, the New Year's Eve party was going ahead, and now that David had secured both Michelle's and Emily's attendance, there were still a few things that required finalizing in the morning. While David had yet to give him an exact time at which he planned to return home, he had assured Blake that all three of them would arrive before the party commenced.

After Emily's accident, and although none of his brother's transgressions from the past few days had been forgiven, Blake found himself willing to oblige David in almost anything. He knew how much Emily meant to David, how much that little girl meant to all of them, and he wanted to do all he could to be of assistance. In spite of everything, David was still his brother and during any difficulty, having the love and support of your family was what mattered most.

Although she had tried to hide it well, Blake could tell

that Gwen was grateful for the opportunity to escape his brother's presence. And he couldn't blame her. Since she'd arrived at the mansion, David had set about to manipulate her and threaten her to agree to his devious marriage plan. Gwen had no reason to trust him and had every right to find David's company repulsive. Yet her sympathy for David at the hospital and her show of support by just being there were enough to remind Blake of her exceptionally kind heart.

The long drive home together had also given them the chance to bring each other up to speed about their blackmail predicament. Blake had been quick to reveal that he'd managed to tell Michelle of David's threats before Emily's accident, but was surprised that Gwen was already aware of it. It was then Gwen informed him about her conversation with Michelle and her earlier discovery during the discussion with David. The new information led them to believe three things. One, that his brother could be a maniacal, egotistical ass; two, that Gwen was essentially free from the confines of David's blackmail and three, that Michelle and David stood a strong chance of reuniting. The only problem was that he and Gwen had no more cards to play. Though they had tried their best, it had essentially been Emily who had brought Michelle and David back together, and now it was up to the two of them to make the next move. It was clear they both still loved each other—they just had to find the courage to put aside their pride and admit it to themselves and each other.

"Are you okay?" Gwen's soft voice cut through the depth of Blake's thoughts.

He glanced up at where she stood at the top of the marble staircase. A puzzled expression furrowed his brow and then he realized that his body had stopped moving at the foot of the stairs.

He offered her a small smile. "Sorry, love. My mind is elsewhere."

Her expression became sweet and endearing as she

hurried back down the stairs to his side.

"Come on," she told him as she linked her arm through his. "Let's get you ready for bed."

Blake smirked. "Miss Deveraux," he said, feigning shock. "Are you trying to take advantage of me?"

Gwen rolled her eyes at him and gave him a quick kiss on the cheek. "I'm sure you'd like that."

He chuckled. Though he wouldn't say no to that kind of opportunity, what Blake wanted more than anything else was to make love to her and to have Gwen agree to be his forever.

At a sudden realization, all of Blake's tiredness disappeared and his mental mistiness cleared. With Michelle having agreed to thwart all of David's plans for blackmail, he and Gwen were now able to be together without fear of backlash or reprisal. After days of keeping their distance to save Gwen's career, here they were, finally alone together, with nothing standing in their way.

He grinned down at her and, in one quick movement, he swept her up into his embrace.

"Whoa! What are you doing?" Her arms wrapped behind his neck as though she was hanging on for dear life.

He laughed again and carried her up the stairs. Though she protested with playful enthusiasm, he refused to put her down. At the closed door of her guest room, he slowly dropped her feet to the floor, but he didn't let her go.

"What's gotten into you?" She giggled as she stared up at him.

With a short step forward, Blake cornered her against the door. As he stared into her gorgeous, green eyes, he cupped her face and tilted her chin to give him better access to her luscious lips. For a brief moment, he kissed his mouth to hers.

Gwen's eyes closed and her body melted against his. But when she moved to deepen the kiss, he stopped her. Her eyes snapped open in surprise.

Blake felt his expression turn serious. "Gwen, I don't want to force you into anything. I'm nothing like my brother. I want you to know that you can say no to me. I might not like it, but I'll respect it."

Tilting her head as if thinking, she narrowed her eyes at him. A warm smile suddenly brightened her beautiful features and she reached out a hand to run her fingers through his dark hair.

"When it comes to you, Blake, I think I've said *no* long enough. I've already wasted too many moments regretting past choices and I'm not about to let another opportunity pass me by."

Surprised by her words, Blake snatched her hand from his hair and placed a kiss to her palm. He smiled.

"I couldn't have said it better myself, love."

Gwen grinned and threw her arms around his neck. Pressing her lips to his, she kissed him so ardently that it nearly took his breath away.

Overwhelmed and exhilarated by her enthusiasm, Blake was almost giddy. His intense love for her was so powerful. He had never believed he could have felt this way about anyone. Then she came along, this magical Gwen Deveraux, and showed him that true love was possible, after all.

***

Inside her room, Gwen kicked her ballet flats to where Blake had left his loafers. Then she dragged him over to the bed. Blake chuckled at her eagerness as she pushed him backward, forcing him to sit on the mattress. Gwen couldn't help but grin at the similarity to their last sexual encounter. But this time, she was the one in control.

Suggestively, she raised her left hand and made Blake watch as she removed David's engagement ring with her mouth. Stealing it from her lips with her fingers, she tossed it over her shoulder.

"Goodbye, blackmail. Hello, Blake." Her tone was all anticipation and desire.

Gwen took his face in her hands and bent her head to him, kissing him passionately. But when his hands went to her waist, drawing her closer, she pulled away.

She wagged her index finger at him. "No, no. It's my turn."

He chuckled. "You're so bossy," he told her with mischievous flirtation.

Ignoring him, she set to work undoing his shirt buttons. But it only took a moment for his disobedience to return. Blake's naughty fingers slithered up her smooth thighs, raising the material of her black mini-dress to her hips. She tried to give him a stern expression as she teasingly batted away his hands. Snatching them, she moved them behind his back, holding them there as she straddled his legs.

As her face neared his, Blake tried to steal a kiss, but she stopped him again.

"Patience," she told him, feigning her best teacher voice. A smirk teased at her lips.

He laughed at her, but obeyed.

Trusting his hands to remain where they were this time, Gwen grabbed the hem of her dress and slipped it off and over her head. She threw it across the room.

Blake's gaze drifted over her body, drinking in the sight of her curves in her lacy, black lingerie.

Gwen felt herself smile. She took immense pleasure in the fact that she could have the same effect on him as he had on her.

Her hands returned to his shirt and as she undid his final button, she felt his fingers grasp her derrière. Playfully, she pushed them back to his sides.

"You really should behave yourself, Mr. Davenport." Her strong words were undermined by a girlish giggle.

Blake grinned. "Or what, Miss Deveraux?"

She smirked and slid a hand beneath her. Through the

tight fabric of his jeans she stroked his bulging erection. He sighed with pleasure and his dark, lustful gaze bore into hers.

Gwen slid her hand up his muscular chest to his open collar. She freed him of his shirt, throwing it in the direction of her dress and then set to work on his jeans.

Blake watched her every move intently, his mouth opening in a silent gasp each time her fingers brushed over his hard shaft.

Slipping from his lap, she tugged his jeans and boxers down his body, baring his sizeable erection as she did so. She yanked them free of his bare feet and threw his clothes behind her.

As she took in the sight of him, naked in front of her, she couldn't help but stare. He was a breathtakingly handsome man of Adonis proportions, with taut muscles in places she hadn't even realized existed. The sight of his enormous erection made her insides quiver with excitement, while his smoldering stare held her captivated.

With a wicked grin, she knelt before him. Her hands slid slowly, sensually up his thighs. When they reached their destination, he shuddered. His breath slipped out in a harsh sigh and his hands dug deep into the bed.

Gwen's grin widened. She was pleased that she could have this kind of effect on him.

Smoothing her fingers around his hard shaft, Gwen held him firmly in her palm. In a slow, teasing motion she moved her hand up and down.

Blake sighed, his eyes closing and teeth clenching as his head fell back in pleasure.

Continuing her rhythm, Gwen dipped her head and closed her lips around him.

Blake groaned at the sensation.

In swirling strokes, she caressed him with her tongue, sucking just slightly as she licked the tip. Sneakily, she slid her free hand deeper between his thighs, fondling the hefty package she found there.

Blake gasped at her touch and his eyes flew open.

Gwen stared up at him from her devious mission and caught his eyes.

His gaze was dark and smoldering as he watched her.

She arched an eyebrow, as if to warn him of her coming mischief. Then, while he stared, she drew the whole length of him into her mouth.

Blake sucked in a breath and his thighs tensed around her.

Gwen held his gaze as she slid her mouth up and down his shaft, her lips mirroring the rhythm of her hand. She sucked him in deeply, then slipped her lips to his tip, her tongue twirling around teasingly before she devoured him again.

Unable to hold her gaze, Blake groaned and let his head fall back.

Gwen quickened her rhythm, up and down, faster and faster. Her mouth made sweet love to his hot, hard, handsome erection.

"Ah," Blake groaned, his breath ragged. "You're driving me crazy, love."

Excitement filled her at the power she had. Gwen was thrilled she could make him feel the ecstasy he'd made her feel. Ever since he'd given her such incredible pleasure, she'd been desperate to return the favor.

While her hand followed her mouth in its seductive dance, her other hand, between his legs, gently kneaded. She felt him tense, the muscles in his thighs contracting around her as her mind-boggling rhythm increased.

As she sucked him in ever so deeply, Blake groaned and threw his head back once more. The warm, salty taste of his liquid desire burst down the back of her throat.

Gwen swallowed with utter satisfaction and slipped her lips slowly from the length of his shaft.

Blake's dark gaze met hers again and he shook his head at her slightly, as if in amazement.

Climbing to her feet, she stood proudly before him and

licked her lips.

"Aren't you glad you behaved yourself, Mr. Davenport?" She made her voice sweet and flirtatious.

Blake's eyes narrowed at her, capturing her gaze.

Gwen stared at the sexy promise in his eyes, feeling elated that she had succeeded in her mission. But her distraction made her vulnerable and Blake's hands were around her waist before she could stop him.

"Now, it's my turn to play, Miss Deveraux." His voice was an erotic growl.

He pulled her on top of him, his mouth capturing hers in a hungry kiss.

At first, she fought him. She had been enjoying being the one with all the power, for once. Then as his kiss deepened, his tongue turning her mind to mush as it danced erotically with hers, she relaxed against him.

Her soft body met the hard, muscular line of his and his stunning erection returned, pressing against her most sensitive region. Gwen gasped into their kiss as a pleasurable, tingling sensation burst through her body. She was already hot and wet between her legs, her insides aching for him. She had never wanted anyone so much.

Taking advantage of her vulnerability once again, Blake rolled on top of her, pinning her to the mattress. His kisses devoured her mouth with a passionate intensity while his hands roamed over her sensitive curves. Sliding a hand beneath her back, he unclipped her lacy, strapless bra with unusual skill and tossed it aside. Then his hand slipped lower. Wasting no time, he tore her panties from her body.

"Hey!" Gwen's voice was husky as she teased him with protest.

Blake's grin was devilish. "You won't be needing these."

He tossed her panties toward the pile of other unwanted clothes. Then he gazed down at her in all her naked glory, his expression a mixture of lustful hunger and absolute marvel.

Gwen felt her cheeks flush under his stare. No one had ever looked at her with so much desire, with so much love. It filled her insides with more than just a sexual pleasure; it filled her with an immense warmth, a passionate love she knew was extraordinary and true.

With a muscular thigh, he parted her legs and pressed himself against her. Gwen moaned at the sensation as his erection slid against her sensitive core. Blake captured her mouth once more, kissing her with intense intimacy before tracing a line of hot, wet kisses down her neck.

Gwen wrapped her legs around him, gasps escaping her lips at the feeling of his gentle mouth on her sensitive flesh. She pressed her hips to his, savoring the sensation of his hard body rubbing against her.

Blake groaned at her movement, pausing for a moment before dipping his head to her chest. He kissed her taut nipples attentively, licking and nipping at her soft skin. Hungry for more, Gwen arched toward him, desperate to feel the caress of his lips.

A sly chuckle, rich and erotic, slipped from Blake's throat and he captured her mouth again. Shifting his body, Blake let the hot, thick length of him slip between her thighs.

Gwen moaned in ecstasy as he entered her, completing her. After spending so long, craving him, yearning for him, she found the sensation utterly mind-blowing.

Blake's tongue seduced her mouth as he moved his hips gently against her in slow, rhythmic thrusts.

Gwen's fingers, clutching at his back, slipped up the nape of his neck and into his hair.

He groaned into their kiss and then, between thrusts, he slipped a hand between them.

Gwen cried out as his fingers flicked over her sensitive nub, caressing it, building her pleasure until she thought she might explode. Her heart raced and she struggled to catch her breath. Her whole body felt on fire.

Thrusting deeper inside her, Blake quickened his

delicious pace and his breathing became ragged.

Gwen held him closer, her legs gripping him to her as she lost herself to the passion. Her hands slipped down to grasp his muscular buttocks as her hips ground against his, matching his rhythm.

Suddenly, the pleasure was all too unbearable. With a final, deep thrust, Blake groaned and Gwen cried out as her body burst in an explosion of warm, tingling fireworks. Her whole body vibrated with an intense ecstasy of which she'd never known.

After catching his breath, Blake gently withdrew, causing her body to shudder with pleasure. Gwen gasped at the delectable sensation. He rolled beside her, their bodies still entangled. Hugging her close, Blake nuzzled his face into her neck.

"I never want to let you go," he whispered to her.

Still trying to catch her breath and waiting for the feeling to return to her legs, Gwen smiled. She turned her head to look at him. His sexy smile displayed his satisfaction, but the look in his dark gaze was pure love.

He kissed her gently and then stared deep into her eyes.

"I think I'm helplessly in love with you, Miss Deveraux," he told her.

She smiled at him contentedly. "I'm in love with you, too, Mr. Davenport."

CHAPTER TWENTY-ONE

From the shade of the balcony, Gwen watched Blake as he gave instructions to the staff from Best Events. They had arrived shortly after ten to begin setting up for the New Year's Eve party that night.

Though Gwen knew Blake would be preoccupied organizing David's party for a few hours, she still couldn't let him out of her sight. She felt almost as though she was lost in a perfect fantasy, with the man of her dreams, and that in letting him out of her sight, the fantasy would surely end.

Gwen doubted she had ever been so happy. She was full of such love and elation just in thinking of him that she felt as if she could cry out in delight.

Blake glanced up at her from where he stood beside the pool house, discussing matters with the party planner. He grinned when he saw Gwen watching him, his expression reflecting the joy of hers. With an affectionate wink, he reluctantly turned his attention to the task he'd promised his brother he'd complete.

Gwen sighed in contentment.

Since first making love last night they hadn't been able to keep their hands off each other. They'd ravished one another twice more before sleep and then once again upon waking. Blake's seemingly innocent suggestion of a shower together had only led to further carnal delights.

Gwen's eyes closed at the pleasurable memory of Blake's talented mouth teasing her sensitive flesh, then the hard, wet length of him filling her so exquisitely, as her moans echoed in the steam-filled room.

Just the thought of it turned her nipples hard, her desire leaving her tingling as moisture pooled between her thighs. Gwen bit her lower lip and opened her eyes.

Blake watched her from across the pool. His dark stare seemed to hold an intimate understanding.

Gwen felt her face flush under his seductive gaze and was almost relieved when his intense stare was disrupted by the approach of another Best Events staff member. Releasing a deep, steadying breath, Gwen tried to control herself. Had they not been interrupted, she would surely have run down the steps to pounce on him. She hadn't realized how difficult it would be to restrain herself in public. Even though they had already shared unimaginable pleasure, her whole body still yearned for more. She couldn't seem to get enough of him. Blake was her drug of choice and she was obviously addicted, with no chance of rehabilitation.

When Gwen dared to glance up at him again, she noticed him do the same. Blake stole a look at her every opportunity he had and it made her smile. It seemed as though they were addicted to each other. The realization filled Gwen with a joyful satisfaction. Perhaps, like her, Blake was afraid to gaze away for too long, in the fear she might just dissolve into nothing but a dream. The thought made her giggle. With all their similarities, they really did seem destined for each other.

It was after one in the afternoon and Gwen had dragged herself away from her role as spectator of the party preparations in order to search for Margaret. As she made her way into the entry, aware that Margaret had last been at the other end of the mansion, the doorbell chimed.

Since she was already there and assuming it to be more people to add to the celebration's organization, Gwen opened the door. To her surprise, it was little Emily with her arm still bandaged and in a sling. The bruise on her forehead had darkened to a deeper shade of purple, but the grin on her sweet face proved it was no longer a bother.

In seeing Gwen, Emily squealed and ran to her. "Miss D!"

Thrilled to see her in a happier situation, Gwen knelt down and wrapped Emily in a gentle hug.

"How's my brave little Emily doing?" she asked tenderly.

Emily excitedly pulled free from her embrace and began to tell her all about her wondrous morning. Apparently, they had already gone to the zoo *and* had ice cream.

Nodding at her story, Gwen giggled at the small child's enthusiasm. Emily was such an adorable child.

It was then Gwen noticed David and Michelle, watching them intently from the landing outside.

Following Gwen's gaze, Emily paused her story and spun around to grab her father's hand.

"Didn't we, Daddy? And there were lions!"

David chuckled at his daughter affectionately. It was a kind, joyful sound Gwen had never thought David could be capable of.

"Yes, yes, honey. We did. There were." David spoke over Emily's further description of their adventures at the zoo.

As if trying to give her ex-husband an opportunity to speak freely, Michelle gently grabbed Emily's other hand and bent down to talk to her.

"Emily baby, why don't we go outside and look at

Daddy's pool?"

Emily nodded with such eagerness that her white-blond curls were left bouncing. With a cute but distracted goodbye to Gwen, Emily released her father's hand and disappeared down the hallway with her mother.

David smiled after them for a moment and then closed the front door behind him. Suddenly his expression became serious.

"How are things here?" His voice was gruff and rather abrupt.

Not appreciating his tone in the slightest, Gwen glared at him.

"Everything has gone to plan, thanks to your very competent brother."

David nodded. "Good."

He stepped around her and then stopped, as if remembering something. When he turned back to face her, his expression was unreadable.

"I don't apologize often, but in this case, Michelle has helped me recognize that I am at fault. I am sorry, Gwen, for everything I have put you through since you arrived at my door. It was wrong of me to treat you in such a way and I wish you to know that any threats I may have made are now forgotten and any inappropriate proposals are no longer valid."

Gwen frowned. Had she actually heard him right? David Davenport was genuinely apologizing for his behavior? She was utterly astounded.

"Thank you." The words slipped through her lips almost from habit.

David nodded curtly and then turned to leave.

All of a sudden, Gwen remembered something and she quickly stopped him.

He looked at her with patient confusion as she struggled to find the right words. "The ring," she told him. "I've left it on your desk in the study."

David's face softened slightly and a small smile spread

his lips.

"I appreciate that," he told her, his tone surprisingly sincere.

It was Gwen's turn to nod.

Before he turned to leave, David leaned a little closer to her.

"My brother is in love with you," he said. "Don't break his heart."

And with that he left her, disappearing down the hallway after his child and her mother.

With a sigh, Gwen giggled. "What a strange family I have found myself a part of."

CHAPTER TWENTY-TWO

Wearing another one of her own stylish dresses, this time a modest, red mini with matching kitten heels, Gwen stood at the heart of the celebration.

Guests had begun arriving before the sun had even set, but this time there was a chirp of young voices each time the front door opened. Though some of David's original guests had declined their invitations upon discovering his new party plans, the majority of his previous invitees were pleased with the opportunity to bring their little ones along.

Children of different ages, along with their parents, filled the enormous recreation room at the back of the mansion. Party games of all kinds were taking place in every corner. There were video games and a mock-up indoor bowling alley to the right, pin the tail on the donkey, and pass the parcel to the left. Even outside, the swimming pool was full of children making use of inflatable animals and there was a piñata by the pool house. As with the Christmas party, the outdoor areas were lit with millions of tiny, colorful lights creating a picturesque, enchanted fairyland. David had even arranged a playhouse, complete with slippery slide, on the grassy area beside the pool and there was a huge jumping castle on the lawn on the adjacent side of the mansion.

In the dining room, there were trays of sandwiches, sausage rolls, mini-pizzas, and various other party foods covering every table. There were plastic fishbowls full of potato chips, colorful sweets, and strategically placed fruit. There were tiers of quiches and other savory treats, and an enormous cupcake tower stood in the center.

As she took it all in, Gwen shook her head in disbelief. It was though David had created every young child's fantasy. In hearing the squeals of enjoyment and the bursts of laughter from all around her, Gwen could tell that Emily's father had succeeded in his celebration plans.

Gwen jumped suddenly as gentle hands slipped between her arms and wrapped around her waist. As she glanced back, Blake cuddled her against his body.

"You look stunning," he whispered into her ear.

She giggled. "This party outfit has nothing on the last one."

Gwen grinned at the thought. She couldn't possibly look as beautiful as she had at Christmas. That night, she had been in a gorgeous green gown and had her hair and makeup done by a professional. This time, her dress was her own, her hair was free in a wavy mess, and she'd spent no more than a moment to brush on some mascara and paint on some lipstick.

Blake gazed at her lovingly. "Even better," he told her. "This time you are how you should be. Just as *you*. And I can't imagine anything more incredible."

He planted a soft, affectionate kiss to her lips and Gwen felt as if she might swoon, had he not been holding her steady.

There were a couple of gagging noises and childish moans from the tiny crowd around them and Gwen found herself giggling out of their kiss.

"Okay, okay," she teased as she glanced around at the little kids in front of them. "But you should know that I like boy germs."

"Eew!" It was said by their small crowd with tremendous enthusiasm.

They all cackled playfully at their declaration, giggling at each other's look of disgust.

"Bet he doesn't like girl germs," a little boy at the front piped up.

The boys around him agreed.

"Yeah!"

"As if!"

Gwen laughed at them, their innocence and natural cheekiness filling her heart with warmth and joy.

Blake grinned down at them, his arms still tightly wrapping Gwen in an embrace from behind. He gave them a little shrug.

"Sorry, boys, but I'm a big fan of girl germs." As he spoke, he laid a light kiss on her cheek.

Gwen smiled as the children continued in their humorous sounds of juvenile outrage and revulsion. They were hilariously dramatic.

A sudden loud *thud* noise from outside drew everyone's attention. Startled, then excited the children in front of them squealed and hurried outside to discover the cause of the commotion.

Gwen gave Blake a puzzled look.

He furrowed his brow in confusion and released her just enough to take her hand and lead her outside. Most of the crowd from inside followed suit, as did those around the pool.

The loud noise continued. *Thud, thud, thud.* Almost like a tapping. Then, as they rounded the corner and onto the large, green lawn, Gwen realized what it was.

David was standing on the edge of the empty jumping castle with a microphone in hand. Like the Pied Piper, children flocked to him and sat on the lawn in front of him.

"Hello, everyone," he said cheerfully into the

microphone as the rest of the crowd gathered before him.

Many of the young guests sang out his name in a drawn-out greeting.

"Hello, Mr. Davenport."

He smiled down at them.

"I wonder if you can help me with something?" He spoke to them with an excited tone and wide eyes.

A sea of nodding heads ensued.

Gwen glanced up at Blake, unable to wipe the smile off her face as she did so.

"What's your brother doing?"

He shook his head and looked down at her. His expression was all astonishment.

"I have no idea."

As Blake returned his gaze to David, Gwen followed suit. David was acting peculiarly out of character and she hadn't the slightest idea why.

"Okay," David said enthusiastically. "Now does everyone here know Emily D's mummy?"

There was a gurgle of agreement and more nodding.

"Good. Can you help me find her?"

Children everywhere spun around, searching for Michelle. Though it was early evening and full dark, their task was made slightly easier in the bright glow of the fairy lights strung throughout the trees.

"I found her," a little girl cried out, over to the left. It was Emily.

With a huge grin and using the hand of her uninjured arm, she tried to pull her mother through the crowd.

"Come on, Mommy," she demanded cheerfully as she dragged Michelle before David.

As Gwen looked on, she was surprised to see that Michelle looked a little bit embarrassed.

When she arrived at the foot of the jumping castle, the crowd cheered. Michelle offered them a meek wave and then glanced up at David. He reached a hand out to her.

"Join me," he told her.

Kicking off her heels, she obliged him. Though it was a slight effort to climb atop the bouncing structure with her dignity intact, she managed very well. As the young crowd giggled at the funny adults trying to steady themselves on the bouncing castle, Michelle and David seemed to share a laugh.

Finally, holding hands to help keep each other steady, David became more serious. He turned to her and spoke through the microphone.

"Michelle. You are the loving mother of my magnificent daughter."

He glanced down quickly and winked at Emily before he continued.

"You are a keen businesswoman with a strong will and determined dedication that is unmatched. You are the most stunningly beautiful woman I have ever seen and you excel at everything you do."

Michelle's face softened with emotion as she listened and her free hand went to her heart.

"Michelle, you are perfection. You are the love of my life."

At David's words, the adult guests gasped and Michelle's hand covered her mouth in surprise.

"I am ashamed that it has taken me so long to realize this," David continued. "I'm sorry I wasn't the wonderful husband you deserved when we first married. I'm sorry I didn't meet all your expectations, that I let you down, and that I didn't put our family first when I should have. But I can recognize my faults and I can change."

As he took a wobbly knee on the jumping castle floor before her, the entire crowd was abuzz with noise.

"Michelle," David said as he held her hands in his. "Will you do me the honor of going on a *second* first date?"

From where Gwen stood, it looked as though Michelle was crying. But if anything, they were tears of joy.

She bent down in front of David, murmuring a "yes" into the microphone.

There was a unanimous cheer and resounding claps of approval.

Michelle dropped to her knees before David and threw her arms around him. But her weight on the jumping castle's floor returned the motion and caused them both to lose balance. As they bounced deeper inside the structure, Emily struggled up and inside after them. The kids at the front seemed to see this as their opportunity to resume their jumping castle joy and were quick to follow.

Blake laughed heartily at the sight of his brother and Michelle trying to share a passionate kiss while a swarm of rowdy children bounced alongside them.

"I definitely didn't see that coming," he told Gwen.

She wrapped her arms around him and hugged him close. With a brief kiss to his lips, she grinned at him.

"I guess this proves that love—even the craziest kind—really can conquer all."

With a nod, Blake chuckled.

"I think you're right," he told her.

Then he glanced back at his brother and ex-sister-in-law, struggling to stand up as a multitude of children jumped around them, and he burst out laughing.

Gwen followed his gaze and giggled.

With a grin, he cuddled her even closer.

"But it seems that even love can't conquer a bouncy castle."

CHAPTER TWENTY-THREE

Though it was nearly midnight, many of the younger partygoers and their adult escorts had retired early. Only the adolescent children and their parents remained to enjoy the somewhat subdued celebration, with many of them remaining inside to play video games or Marco Polo in the pool.

From where she relaxed on the outdoor lounge on the terrace beside the canal, Gwen admired the sight of the Davenports' luxury yacht adorned with thousands of colorful lights. It cast a romantic glow across the water, giving the night a dreamlike atmosphere.

Across the canal, she could see other lively parties taking place, both in the magnificent mansions and on the water, in moored sea craft. She could hear yelling and playful screams drifting across the placid waves, similar to those coming from the mansion behind her.

She sighed in contentment. It seemed everyone around was enjoying their New Year's Eve as much as she was.

Though she might have suffered a great deal over the last few days, bewildered and frightened by emotional and mental turmoil as well as by physical blackmail, everything had changed for the better. Her career was safe, she didn't have to marry the wrong brother, and she had met a man who utterly completed her. Now at the end of it all, it seemed as though she had actually enjoyed her festive week at the Davenports' mansion. Or at least no longer regretted agreeing to the invitation. For if she hadn't agreed, she would have never met Blake.

"There you are, love." Blake's voice came from the stairs leading up to the pool.

"Here I am," she told him.

"You disappeared on me." He chuckled as he made his way over to her.

She smiled at him. "I wanted to give you some space while you spoke to David. I thought you deserved some brotherly time after his grand proposal, earlier."

Blake laughed. "It certainly was a spectacle."

When he reached her, Gwen grabbed his arm and pulled him down to sit on the cushion beside her. She snuggled into him. Though she fought it, tiredness was slowly overtaking her.

Blake wrapped his arms around her shoulders and hugged her against his chest.

"You know," he began slowly, as if choosing his words carefully.

Gwen nodded against him.

"You don't have to leave tomorrow if you don't want to."

With tired eyes, she glanced up at him.

Blake smiled down at her and brushed a stray curl behind her ear.

"I mean, I've spoken to David. He's happy for you to stay..." His voice trailed off and his smile widened.

Gwen frowned and tried to finish his sentence. "Another couple of days."

"Indefinitely." The word burst from Blake's lips like a secret he could no longer contain.

Gwen's eyes widened and she sat up. She wasn't tired anymore. "Are you being serious?" Her tone was incredulous.

He laughed at her. "That wasn't exactly the response I'd been expecting."

She shook her head, as if trying to come to terms with his offer.

"Sorry. It's just—yes, of course. But do you really mean that?"

Blake grinned and pulled her back down into his arms. "Of course I do."

Resting her head against the warm of his taut, muscular chest, Gwen listened to him over the gentle beat of his heart.

"Now that David and Michelle are giving their relationship another go, he plans to spend the rest of January down in Brisbane. He believes they are all in need of some exceptional family time."

Gwen felt herself nod. Trust David to make such an understatement. But she had to give him credit for trying. After all, he had gone to a great deal of trouble, putting all of his pride aside, to ask Michelle for a second chance. He might not have been brother of the year, even brother of the century, but she had to admit that he wasn't all bad.

Blake stroked her arm affectionately as he rested his head on top of hers.

"He's told me he'd like me to look after the place in his absence. So, I thought—if you wanted to—that you could keep me company."

Though his words were precise, the nervous lilt to his voice suggested he was ever so slightly afraid she might turn down his offer.

"Don't you want to be cooped up in this big house all alone?" Gwen giggled as she teased him.

He tickled her gently in the ribs and she let out a little squeal.

"That's what you get for cheekiness," he laughed.

"Okay." She conceded to him as she tried to catch her breath.

Gwen gazed up into his dark eyes and offered him a delighted smile.

"I'd love to keep you company," she said.

His grin showed his relief and his elation.

"Excellent. Perhaps then, even after January you might consider staying with me?"

Gwen frowned. "Here?"

"Actually…" he said the word a little sheepishly. "I have a house up on the Noosa hill. I usually rent it out during the holidays, as David prefers me to stay here."

Gwen felt her jaw drop in shock.

"You have a secret house?"

He chuckled. "It's not a secret, Gwen. It's *my* house. I only stay here for the holidays because David enjoys having family around."

Looking deep into her eyes, Blake's expression once again became a bit shy.

"It's a beautiful house," he told her. "A large house. I'd definitely say it was big enough for two."

He paused, staring down at her, watching her reaction intently.

"I think you'd really like it there."

She quirked an eyebrow at him.

"My, Mr. Davenport," she said, feigning surprise. "Is that your way of asking me to move in with you?" Gwen giggled at her silliness. She wasn't certain that was what he had planned, but she couldn't help but tease him.

Turning serious, Blake shook his head.

"No, Gwen," he said. "I'm asking you something much more important."

An eruption of noise from the mansion behind them startled them both. As they glanced up, barely able to distinguish the commotion in the pool area above them, a loud counting started.

"It's almost midnight." Gwen's voice was breathy with excitement.

"Five!" It was a screamed countdown.

From where they sat, they could even hear their neighbors across the canal.

"Four!"

Blake stared at Gwen and a contented smile brightened his face.

"Three," he yelled, joining in on the din.

"Two!" Gwen wasn't about to let him count alone.

"One!" They shouted the word in unison and laughed.

"Happy New Year." Blake's voice dropped an octave lower and his dark eyes pierced into hers.

As he leaned closer to her, his lips nearly touching hers, Gwen felt her whole body tingle in anticipation. Cupping her cheek with his warm hand, his thumb caressed her skin.

"Happy New Year." Her voice was husky as her gaze dropped to his mouth.

In a breath, Blake's mouth covered hers. His kiss was filled with all of his desire for her. It was hungry and loving, ardent and teasing. It was so overwhelming, so breathtaking, that Gwen felt as though she could swoon in his arms.

When his lips finally left hers, it took her a moment to gather her thoughts and flutter her eyes open.

Blake gazed down at her, his expression full of satisfaction and affection.

"Gwen," he said to her. "Marry me."

Gwen's eyes snapped open and her jaw dropped.

"Yes!" The word left her lips as if they had a mind of their own.

Blake was utterly overjoyed at her answer. Grinning with elation, he dropped to his knee in front of her. Holding her hand in his, he reached his free hand behind him for a moment. It returned with a tiny, intricately carved, wooden box.

"This was my grandmother's," he said. "I promised her that I'd give it to the woman who completed me. The one, who once I'd met, I couldn't live without."

Blake opened the box carefully.

Again, Gwen felt herself gasp. It was the most beautiful piece of jewelry she'd ever seen. A glittering square cut diamond perched atop the stunning gold band, while a duo of smaller emeralds sat either side.

"Blake—" Gwen was totally lost for words.

She couldn't believe that he would offer her something so special, something that meant so much to him and his family. Gwen was completely overwhelmed. She swallowed deeply as she suddenly realized she was beginning to cry.

Leaving the box in her hands, Blake wiped away a tear. He grinned at her.

"These better be tears of joy."

Gwen nodded.

Taking the delicate ring from the box, Blake handed it to her.

"Read the inscription," he said.

Gwen wiped her eyes clear and looked carefully at the inscription. The words left her lips in a whisper. "Two hearts. One soul. Together always." She gazed at him, her heart feeling as though it might burst.

"You are my soul mate, Gwen, just as my grandmother was to my grandfather. I'm sure I knew the moment I met you that we belonged together. You are the woman of my dreams and I want you to spend the rest of your life with me."

Gwen felt hot tears welling in her eyes once again. She couldn't believe this was happening, that she'd just agreed to marry Blake. It was everything she had come to wish for. It was a complete dream come true.

Nodding at him, Gwen slipped from her seat on the lounge down to straddle his legs. Blake's arms wrapped around her waist as she held her engagement ring between them. Wiping away her tears with the back of her hand, she smiled at him.

"Blake, you complete me," she told him, her words full

of the all-consuming love she felt for him.

He grinned at her, his expression part disbelief.

"I think I knew, too, on the first day I met you, that I loved you." She chuckled at the thought.

"You were brash and controlling as you tried to stop me from making a huge mistake and yet, my heart raced at the sight of you. You told me to go and all I could think of was touching you, kissing you."

Raising her hand, she delicately slipped the ring over her fourth finger. It fit perfectly, as though it belonged there. She caught his eyes with a loving gaze. "You are my soulmate, Blake. I love you and I think I always have."

Cupping his face in her hands, she matched her lips to his and kissed him ardently.

Blake hugged her closer, pressing her curves against his hard body.

From where she straddled his hips, beneath her lacy panties, she could feel his growing erection. Pleasurable sensations whipped through her body, her sensitive insides eager for attention. With a blissful laugh, she broke free of the intimate kiss.

"Oh my, Mr. Davenport," she teased him. "We seem rather pleased with this arrangement, don't we?" She dropped her gaze to his groin and bit her lip seductively.

"Couldn't be happier, Miss Deveraux. Or should I say Mrs. Davenport?"

Blake winked at her and she giggled.

"You can give me whatever title you prefer, Mr. Davenport. Just as long as I'm yours."

Blake gazed at her with absolute infatuation. "Forever and always," he said.

With a hand to her cheek, he captured her lips in an amorous kiss.

Gwen melted into his arms and in that moment she knew the truth. They were a match made in Heaven from the very beginning, destined to be happy together for all of their days.

***

They wed in February in a small ceremony at Winch Cove, with David making use of their reception to re-propose to Michelle.

Less than two months later, the pair of happily married couples met up for Easter, with Gwen quick to announce to Michelle that Emily would soon have a little cousin.

Just shy of October, their daughter Jennifer was born, named especially so in honor of Blake's late grandmother.

Living up to the inscription on the engagement ring, Blake and Gwen remained forever two hearts, one soul, together always.

DON'T MISS THIS AWARD WINNING BOOK BY AUTHOR TAMMY MANNERSLY

*You can't hide from destiny...***This sexy 220+ page contemporary romance novel is guaranteed to have you hooked on Cal and Lucy's *love/hate* relationship until the very end.**

Callum Hawthorne is one of those lucky guys who seem to have it all. He's a wealthy property tycoon, the CEO of his family's company. He's handsome, intelligent and charming and has a gorgeous new woman on his arm every week. But there's one thing still missing – the love of his life, Lucy Spencer.

Fourteen long years ago, Lucy left for college and cut off all contact with Cal, leaving their mutual friend Madison as his only connection. That was until in his effort to save his deceased father's beloved Gold Coast property, The Calypso, Cal contacts Insight Marketing, the best advertising firm in Melbourne, and discovers his Lucy among the team.

Successful marketing executive, Lucy Spencer had

managed to avoid her ex-best friend for nearly half their lives. Fearful of trusting him, loving him and having her heart broken all over again, Lucy tries to keep her distance from him, but discovers that there is a fine line between love and hate, and maybe – just maybe – Cal could be her inescapable destiny.

PERSUADING LUCY is about broken friendships, lost love and the courage to heal all. If you love reading the novels of Mandy Magro and Rachael Johns, then you'll adore this steamy second-chance love story by award-winning author, Tammy Mannersly.

~PERSUADING LUCY, a 1st Place WINNER for the prestigious 2018 CHATELAINE BOOK AWARDS FOR ROMANTIC FICTION, will quickly become your new favorite read!~

REVIEWS
"5 Stars! BEST BOOK"
— Chanticleer Book Reviews

"Friendship is an endearing theme in this well-written, fast-paced novel. It exists in every form, long-time friends, new friends, the kind of friends who will help drown your sorrows in wine, and the kind who will literally and figuratively rescue you from yourself...the entire premise is based upon the friendship of Lucy and Cal, a lasting friendship that holds both love and hate."
— Andrea Murray, Book Reviewer, Chanticleer Book Reviews

FROM THE AUTHOR
Hey lovely readers! Persuading Lucy is my second contemporary romance novel and sits closest to my heart.

As well as being set in two of my favourite locations - Melbourne and the Gold Coast, Australia, the concept for the story is loosely based on real events. It's incredible what destiny has in store for us! While Cal and Lucy's story is one of romance and second chances, Persuading Lucy is also about friendship and what we lose when we leave people behind.

I hope you enjoy reading this enemies-to-lovers romance as much as I loved writing it! Please leave a review and let me know what you think of Cal and Lucy's story - thank you! :-)

ABOUT THE AUTHOR

Tammy Mannersly is an Australian author based in Brisbane, Queensland. She loves writing romance, has a fondness for animals, is crazy about movies and enjoys a great Happily Ever After. Her passion for writing started from a very young age and lead her to complete a Bachelor Degree in Creative Industries majoring in Creative Writing at Queensland University of Technology. You can find out more information about Tammy and her work on her website: www.tammymannersly.com or by visiting Facebook: https://www.facebook.com/profile.php?id=10001372726 8166 and Goodreads: https://www.goodreads.com/user/show/60685325-tammy-mannersly.